P9-AFY-833

FIC
BEN
SEVEN DAY BOOK  91435

Benjamin, Zelda

Brooklyn ballerina

FOX LAKE DISTRICT LIBRARY
255 E. GRAND AVENUE
FOX LAKE, ILLINOIS 60020

BROOKLYN
BALLERINA

BROOKLYN BALLERINA

•

Zelda Benjamin

AVALON BOOKS
NEW YORK

© Copyright 2001 by Zelda Piskosz
Library of Congress Catalog Card Number: 00-193455
ISBN 0-8034-9473-4
All rights reserved.
All the characters in this book are fictitious,
and any resemblance to actual persons,
living or dead, is purely coincidental.
Published by Thomas Bouregy & Co., Inc.
160 Madison Avenue, New York, NY 10016

PRINTED IN THE UNITED STATES OF AMERICA
ON ACID-FREE PAPER
BY HADDON CRAFTSMEN, BLOOMSBURG, PENNSYLVANIA

Chapter One

T he sharp pain in Rebecca's right calf sent a wave of spasms through her leg.

"You okay, lady?" the cab driver asked.

"Just a cramp." Determined not to give in to the discomfort, she handed the man his money and stepped onto the sidewalk. A whopping dose of Ibuprofen and some ice would have her in shape for the recital this evening.

Once a week Rebecca traveled from her Manhattan neighborhood back to her old Brooklyn dance school. Hoping to instill her love of the ballet, she helped her mentor teach the local kids some finer points of dance. The little ballerinas assigned to Rebecca had worked so diligently, she would hate to disappoint them.

A group of young women gathered around one of the park benches lining Ocean Parkway. Their baby strollers cluttered the street. They smiled at Rebecca as she maneuvered around their little enclave. She smiled back, envious of their leisure time. Busy studying the babies, she almost ran into a man dressed in the traditional black coat and felt hat of the Hasidim. He rushed forward, paying no attention to Rebecca. This was Brooklyn. Stuck forever in a time warp.

In front of her stood the building that had the power to bring her back to the old neighborhood. She tilted her head for a better view of the sign, LILLIANA'S DANCE ACADEMY. The faded letters were in need of restoration and the D danced on its side.

Rebecca stepped inside the little studio. The heavy oak door grunted its usual welcome. As she walked closer to the stage, muffled voices echoed from behind the curtain. The medley of English, Russian, and Yiddish voices grew louder as Rebecca approached the platform. Her heart skipped a beat. She took a deep breath and prepared for the worst. She knew Lilliana's fresh-off-the-boat accent only surfaced when she was angry or upset. The other voice was not as clear. Who was back there harassing Lilliana?

With little regard for her sore leg, Rebecca climbed the steps two at a time. Fortunately the scene backstage was not as gloomy as she imagined. Lilliana stood face to face with her tall, lanky landlord, Les Morgan.

Without hesitating, Rebecca slipped between them. She looked from Les to Lilliana. "What's going on here?" Rebecca demanded.

"Ask this gonif, this thief." Lilliana shook her finger so close to Les's face it bounced off his pointy nose. "Today he comes to collect the rent."

"Not just this month's. She's six months overdue."

"Six months?" Rebecca said.

Lilliana shrugged. "A little detail his father never made a big deal about."

"Why today?" Rebecca shrugged to hide her confusion. "You know we're putting on a recital this evening."

Les Morgan stretched out his arm to touch Rebecca. "I saw your season finale." He let out a sigh of satisfaction. "Exquisite." Then he gestured toward Lilliana. "Too bad this old crow won't be fostering any new prima ballerinas inside the walls of this old building."

"Les Morgan, how dare you be so rude to Lilliana." Rebecca looked at his hand on her elbow, then shook it off. "The woman is a master."

"Master of dance and fool with her money."

Rebecca's glare warned him not to say another word. She wanted to scream at him and scold him for what he was doing to Lilliana. The greedy look in his eyes made her temper soar. "I won't ask you to leave because I want the satisfaction of walking out on you." She pivoted, hoping to look convincing.

Again he reached out to place his arm on her shoulder. "Becky, such harsh words from you."

"You know what Lilliana and the school mean to me." Rebecca turned to face Les.

"I'm sorry you have to be involved."

She felt a moment of panic as thoughts raced through her mind. The school and Lilliana had been part of her life for as long as she could remember. Rebecca turned toward Les. "Can we discuss this later?"

"Not much to talk about, but I'll be back."

Rebecca and Les had been friends a long time. She remembered being six years old and meeting the funny kid who lived next door. The other kids would get annoyed when he tried to impress them with his father's fortune. It never registered until years later how much he was actually worth. However, she knew a side of Les most people would not believe existed. She knew the man who held season tickets to the ballet. After every performance he would show up backstage dressed in a tuxedo, teary-eyed and holding a bouquet of long-stemmed roses with the thorns removed. That was the Les Morgan she would plead with.

"I don't understand why you try to be nice to that greedy monster. He was a mean kid and now he's a nasty adult." Lilliana twisted her hands together. "If we can only find someone willing to stand up to him."

Rebecca brushed a strand of gray hair from Lilliana's forehead. "We'll find someone who understands all this financial mumbo jumbo. Maybe even someone who loves the ballet."

"I hope so." Lilliana sighed. "Even if they don't like the ballet, I'll take their money."

Rebecca put her arms around the older woman and hugged her. "Forget Les. We have a show to put on."

"And too many things to do. Want to pick up the refreshments at Fleichman's Bakery?" Lilliana asked.

"Don't they deliver?"

"This isn't your fancy-shmancy Manhattan neighborhood where you call for a cup of coffee. People do things for themselves here." Lilliana nodded at Rebecca's leg. "Go. A little walk will loosen up your muscles."

The woman noticed everything. Rebecca knew she was more fortunate than most of her colleagues to have received her early training from someone as talented as her old dance master. The technique and discipline that Lilliana instilled in her at an early age were the basic learning experiences Rebecca still carried with her. How did such a talented, devoted woman like Lilliana get the school into such a mess? Rebecca knew she had to put the incident with Les in the back of her mind. Until the recital was over, nothing else mattered.

"If the girls come early, don't work them too hard," Rebecca said over her shoulder. "I don't want anyone to get hurt before the performance."

"You worry too much about your students. Some babies of your own are what you need."

"Lilliana," Rebecca protested, pouting. "I'm not ready to give up my dancing career."

"Go now." Lilliana patted Rebecca's rear as she left.

The gesture made Rebecca smile. Lilliana was more than her teacher. She was her friend. Her heart ached at the possibility of Lilliana having to give up the school. Determined to do whatever was necessary to save the building, she ventured out onto the streets of the old neighborhood.

She looked at the men and women and thought how easily they were attached to the streets, buildings, and people where they lived. Except for the school and Lilliana, Rebecca didn't have very fond memories of this place. As a teenager she had tried to make friends with neighborhood girls. They rushed off to the mall to meet boyfriends while Rebecca agonized over her form and position at the barre. When her family moved to Manhattan so she could attend the ballet company's high school, no one realized she was gone. Except for Les.

She walked a short distance before turning off Ocean Parkway. The shop-lined street mimicked the cultural mix of the neighborhood. Vic's Pizza Place, Liang's Laundry, and Fleichman's Bakery stood in their permanent spots. She glanced in the bakery window. A line of customers snaked in front of the counter, moving in slow motion as they inched closer. Neon numbers flashed on the wall announcing the next to be served. Rebecca hesitated before stepping inside.

"In or out, lady." A shopper already burdened with packages waited for Rebecca to cross the threshold.

As a grown woman of twenty-eight, Rebecca performed on stage with poise and confidence, before hundreds of people. Walking into a crowded bakery should not disturb her. But it did. She hated crowds.

Reluctantly she stepped inside. The yeasty smell of baked bread greeted her. This was Brooklyn. Just like the surrounding streets, not much had changed.

New tables had been scattered along the back wall to give the bakery an updated look, but the people were the same. They wore familiar expressions of satisfaction as they devoured crusty rolls and sweet buns. The hiss of the cappuccino machine replaced the old percolator. Some of the men wore baseball jerseys, Fleichman's Bombers written across their chests. In the past they might have worn bowling shirts or been reading the racing track forms. Today they spoke with authority on the Mets' latest pitching trade while they gave her licentious glances over steamy cups of mocha.

Behind the counter a dark-haired man casually looked in her direction. Beneath his apron the fabric of his baseball shirt stretched over taut muscles.

"Number seventy-two," the bakery lady shouted. A few gray strands escaped her hair net.

Those around her looked at their tickets. No one stepped forward. No one answered.

Rebecca uncrumpled the green ticket in her hand—number ninety-two. There were twenty people ahead of her. She suddenly had an idea. She waited for the number to be called again.

Once more the lady shouted, "Number seventy-two."

As the bakery lady reached for the next number, Rebecca inched her way to the front of the line. She took a deep breath and in a loud firm voice announced, "Number seventy-two." She tossed her number ninety-two into the basket with the other discarded tickets.

The bakery lady raised a bushy gray brow. "Can I help?"

The counterman interrupted the older woman. "I'll wait on this one, Bubbe."

The deep male voice caught Rebecca off guard. His mouth twitched with amusement. Rebecca flushed when she realized he might be wise to her little trick. Conscious of his scrutiny from the moment she had entered the bakery, Rebecca knew she'd been caught. She wanted to look away. Yet she couldn't help examining him.

Tall and slender, he stood in contrast to the short stout ladies with whom he shared counter duties. Sharp chiseled features hid under his day-old stubble. His looks favored the hero in a classic ballet.

"Can I help you?"

Too mortified to do more than nod, she handed him Lilliana's shopping list.

He read the list out loud. "Two dozen assorted danish, three pounds of cookies, bagels and a mandel bread."

"The order should have been called in yesterday." Rebecca's voice returned. "It's for Miss Lilliana's Academy."

The counterman indicated by a nod that he was aware of the order. He turned and walked away, but not before surveying her with a slanted look.

Rebecca studied the cakes and pastries in the case. She looked up to find the counterman staring at her. A playful smile curved his lips.

Rebecca found it difficult not to acknowledge his intriguing gaze. She smiled back. She couldn't resist stealing glances at him as he strutted behind the counter. He might get the wrong idea and think she was flirting with him. If she thought it would expedite her departure she would be willing to try, but encouraging strangers was not her thing. Especially a counterman in a Brooklyn bakery.

Around her the other customers shifted impatiently. "Jake, move a little faster. You can talk to the pretty girls later." A little old lady maneuvered her way to the front of the line.

"Mind if I wait on Mrs. Shapiro while they bag your order?"

"Give the girl a cookie while she's waiting." Mrs. Shapiro, the little old lady, stepped forward. She studied Rebecca over the wire rim of her glasses. "She can use the extra weight."

"Give her two cookies," Bubbe said from the other side of the counter.

Jake reached into the glass case and pulled out a cookie, a bright red cherry sitting in the middle.

"No thanks." Rebecca shook her head to reinforce her refusal.

A ballerina's discipline didn't allow for indulging in sweets. If it had been a piece of the fresh rye bread he sliced for Mrs. Shapiro, Rebecca would have found it difficult to say no. Fresh-baked bread was one of her weaknesses.

Jake popped the cookie in his mouth and walked to the slicing machine. Without missing a piece he transferred the bread from the blades to a crisp white bag. Mrs. Shapiro stretched on her tiptoes. She scattered a few pennies, nickels and dimes on the counter.

Rebecca expected Jake to count the meager change. Instead he reached into his pocket, took out a crisp dollar bill, added it to the coins, then rang up the sale. Mrs. Shapiro tucked her purchase into her worn canvas bag and left. Touched by his kind act, Rebecca wanted to tell him how considerate he was, but no one else seemed to notice.

Anxious to be on her way, Rebecca paid for the baked goods, gathered up her packages, and excused her way through the crowd. Outside the bakery Rebecca stopped for a moment to glance at her watch. It was later than she thought. At the corner the traffic light turned red. With no time to waste, Rebecca stepped off the curb ready to cross against the light.

"Hey lady, watch where ya goin'," the driver of a blue Volkswagen shouted.

She jumped back. Safely on the curb, she redistributed the boxes and bags in her arms. Oh no, she was missing one. She had no one to blame but herself. If she hadn't been in such a hurry to leave the bakery, she wouldn't have to go back.

Rebecca turned. Before she took another step she noticed the counterman running toward her. He held a white bakery box in his hand. His pace was smooth and even, like a well-trained athlete's.

"You forgot this," he said. "Wouldn't want you to be deprived of my grandfather's famous mandel bread."

With her hands full of cumbersome packages Rebecca couldn't balance her bundles. A poppy-seed bagel edged its way out of an overstuffed bag.

Jake caught the bagel as it rolled over the top, placed it back in the bag, and crinkled the brown paper edges tight and secure.

"Thanks," Rebecca said.

"No problem." Jake shifted his weight and hooked his

thumbs in the sides of his apron. "Can I help you carry your bags?"

"No thanks. I'll manage."

Before turning the corner onto Ocean Parkway, Rebecca glanced over her shoulder. The counterman stood outside the bakery watching her.

Jake loved Brooklyn. He prided himself in knowing who lived in the few city blocks that defined his old neighborhood. He wondered why he had never seen the woman in the pink leotard before.

He went back into the store. It would be at least another half-hour before the morning crowd started to dwindle. With two countergirls out sick, he couldn't leave his grandmother at the mercy of the weekend shoppers. The guys would just have to wait a little longer for their prize shortstop.

Jake stopped at the table where his teammates stuffed warm rolls and bagels into their mouths. "Take it easy, guys, or those Bensonhurst boys'll run all over us."

"No way. One, two, three, they won't know what hit 'em," the Bombers' enthusiastic pitcher said.

"I hope so. I've got to get to the recital on time. Jewel's dancing a solo," Jake said.

"My kid's dancing too. Not to worry. If I'm a little late, the wife'll be there."

Jake tapped his teammate on the side of his head. "Remember I'm mom and dad to Jewel."

The pitcher rubbed his head. He realized his indiscretion.

"I'm sorry, Jake, I know you're a single dad. You'll get there on time. We'll whip 'em. You'll see."

"Not if I stand here kibitzing with you guys." Jake noticed the line of customers extended out the door.

Back behind the counter Jake's grandmother shot a curious look at him. "She's a pretty lady."

"I don't remember seeing her in here before," Jake said. "Do you know who she is?"

"Why? Are you interested?"

"No, just curious."

"Oh, excuse me, heaven forbid you should think of finding a mother for your daughter."

"I should probably find a wife first."

"That would be a good idea." Bubbe's hand rested on the ticket machine. "Number ninety-two."

Jake smiled. He wondered what number the leotard-clad woman had really had. He followed his grandmother to the cash register. "You didn't answer my question."

"What do you think, I know everyone in Brooklyn?" She rang up her sale. "That will be a dollar ninety-five."

"New cash register?" the customer said.

"Yes. Jake talked us into getting it. My husband loves it. Tells us how much cake and cookies we sell. It does everything but bake the bread. Smart machine. Just like my grandson, real smart."

"You're ignoring me," Jake chided.

At the cappuccino machine Jake's buddy Vinnie filled his cup. "Go ahead, Grandma Fleichman, tell the boy who she is. It isn't every day he asks about a pretty lady."

"Vinnie, fill your coffee cup and sit down," Jake said. "If you're not working, you don't belong behind the counter."

"Don't get nasty. I just think it's time ya start thinking about serious dating again. Ya can't be all business and no pleasure. There are some nice ladies out there. Everyone isn't a witch like your ex."

"Johanna wasn't a witch. She just had her own agenda."

Jake didn't feel this was the time or place to get into a discussion about his failed marriage.

"And it didn't include her husband or kid," Vinnie said.

"Exactly, I've got my daughter to think about."

"No big deal." Vinnie threw his hands in the air. "Find someone who likes kids. It's not hard to fall in love with Jewel, she's a sweetheart."

"Jewel already has a nanny."

"Help me out here, Bubbe. Your grandson is not getting it."

"Such a good-looking boy." Jake's grandmother rubbed her twisted fingers across his cheek. "Whoever falls in love with Jewel gets her handsome father as the bonus. Maybe you should take a little more interest in your daughter's activities."

"I would, Bubbe, if I had the time."

Vinnie set his cup down on the counter and followed Jake to the number machine. "At least admit the lady in the tights ain't bad-looking. Don't disappoint me," he said. "You can't be down on all women. I know you haven't lost your eye for a good-looking broad."

"Not to disappoint you, I can still appreciate a good-looking broad, as you so crudely put it." The lines around Jake's mouth softened. He didn't like friends and family pushing him into the social scene, but he had to admit the woman in the pink leotard was very attractive.

"Good, good, at least you're looking. Only took you six years," Vinnie said in his casual jesting way. "And you did run after her with one of Manny's mandel breads."

Jake put up his hands, warning Vinnie to stop. "She was a customer. I was just being courteous."

"I don't see you running after Mrs. Shapiro with a pumpernickel rye," Vinnie chided. "Come on, we've got a ballgame to play."

Chapter Two

The music started and Miss Lilliana ushered the first group of young dancers onto the stage. The audience was gracious. Their applause offered encouragement to the tiny novice performers. Rebecca and her students won a standing ovation for their snappy jitterbug. The grande finale, a solo by Rebecca, brought the audience to their feet in a hand-clapping furor as she whirled round in a series of pirouettes.

After the recital, students and their guests gathered in the great room. Miss Lilliana ushered Rebecca toward the proud parents and grandparents at the refreshment table.

Rebecca paused. She noticed the man from the bakery mingling in the crowd. Shaved and changed into jeans and a shirt, he was even more attractive than earlier.

Parents rushed forward to praise Lilliana. Rebecca found

herself surrounded by her students' families. She lost sight of the bakeryman as she was bombarded with thank-yous for taking the time from her busy schedule to work with the neighborhood children.

"I enjoyed teaching them." Rebecca leaned against the table for support. "They were such enthusiastic students." She was beginning to feel a tingling sensation in her toes. Her leg seemed too sore to hold her up any longer.

"I think Miss Becky did one pirouette too many." Lilliana eased her arm around Rebecca. "She needs to take a little break."

Rebecca ignored the scowl on her mentor's face. She excused herself and limped toward the backstage stairs. She had taken only a few steps when a spasm shot through her leg.

All alone, Rebecca concentrated on easing the pain in her leg. She searched through her satchel for an ice pack. A nearby chair offered her the support she needed. Not far behind her, Lilliana continued to greet the guests.

"It's about time you showed up to see your daughter dance."

Rebecca was curious as to whom Lilliana had made the last remark. Glancing over her shoulder, she noticed the bakery counterman. He laughed and kissed Lilliana on the cheek.

"It's not easy being a single parent."

"No excuses," Lilliana said.

"Got a minute?" The man put his arm around the older woman's shoulder and guided her away from the crowd.

Rebecca wondered what he wanted to say that couldn't be said in front of the rest of the group. Maybe he had heard about the problem with Les and was going to offer to sponsor a bake sale. With short strides she covered the remaining distance to the stairs. She couldn't help but wonder which of the students belonged to him. She almost forgot her pain until she raised her leg to climb the first step.

Once she was safely backstage she concentrated on easing the pain. Again she searched through her satchel for an ice pack. Unable to find one she had to settle for the messy alternative, ice cubes in a plastic bag. Easing herself down into an old wooden chair, she elevated her leg onto an empty crate. Just a few minutes' rest was all she needed.

Les Morgan interrupted her quiet solitude. "There you are." He looked from her ice-wrapped leg to her face. "The old injury?"

Rebecca nodded. "You decided to come back?"

"I wanted to see how many people showed up." Les gave her a sly smile. "And count the profits."

Rebecca repositioned her leg. "There are no profits from a school recital."

She knew Lilliana's devotion to her students sometimes interfered with her judgment. Lilliana had mentioned that enrollment was up but some parents were behind in their payments. Rebecca wondered how much deeper in debt the recital had put the school. "Did you enjoy the recital?"

"As usual." Les ran his finger inside his shirt collar. "Even in this drab setting your performance was rare." Little beads of sweat formed on his forehead.

"Are you okay, Les?"

"It's very warm in here." He fanned himself with the dance program. "Aren't you hot?"

"Of course it's warm. The air conditioning is hardly working." Rebecca removed the ice from her leg and stood up to face him. The bag leaked and formed a little puddle around her foot. "Know anyone interested in paying for the repairs?"

Les took her seat. "You know I'd help out if I could, but the city building department is coming down hard on owners of these old buildings."

"Would you really be willing to help?" Rebecca looked at the magnificent windows. Marked with bubbles and waves, they made the old room bright in spite of its run-down walls and floors.

"I might." Les followed Rebecca's gaze. "It was a nice building once."

"It still is." Rebecca ran her fingers along the cherry-wood window trim. "Lilliana's been here forever."

"I believe you care what happens to Lilliana, but this neighborhood? Come on, Becky. You never looked back once you left." Les hesitated. His eyes scanned the confined space, resting for a moment on the peeling paint and water spots. "But because of our friendship, I'll do what I can. I'll give you some time to work things out. Find a sugar daddy or someone willing to help raise some money."

"Without any conditions?" Rebecca asked. She wanted to believe his generosity was sincere but his reputation preceded him. She wanted to believe his love of the ballet or their friendship was behind his offer.

"Just one." He shrugged.

Rebecca took a deep breath and held it for a minute while she waited to hear the condition of Les's offer.

"I want to know who offers help and how you'll be raising the money." His tone was heavy with doubt.

"You don't think we'll find anyone, do you?"

"I want you to see for yourself that no one would put money into this old building."

"How long do we have?"

"I'd like to give you all the time you'll need but I can't.

These old buildings are money pits. I'll give you until the end of the summer."

"And then what will you do?" she asked him in a low voice tight with anger. "Evict Lilliana?"

His hands reached out to touch her as she walked past. "Don't be angry, Becky. It's business. It has nothing to do with our friendship."

Rebecca did not hear what Les had to say. Lilliana's heavy accent vibrated from the front stage.

"Where is that miserable thief?" Lilliana appeared. "How dare you spread rumors among my customers that the school is closing."

"Now, now, Lilliana, you can't believe I would say anything about your financial troubles. I might have mentioned to one or two people how difficult it is to maintain these old buildings."

"I'm not surprised." Rebecca glared at Les. "You always have your own agenda."

Lilliana patted Rebecca's arm. "Don't worry. I think I've found someone who can help us through all this craziness." She glared at Les. "And you are not going to like who it is."

Ever since Rebecca could remember, Lilliana had a solution to every problem. With the grace and style of a performing dancer, Lilliana parted the curtain for her newfound ally.

In spite of her surprise, she was pleased to see the man from the bakery.

"I don't think you've met my assistant, Rebecca Carr," Lilliana said.

"Jake Fleichman." He fingers closed around Rebecca's hand in a strong grasp. "The lady with the wrong number on her ticket."

"Caught in the act." Rebecca could feel the heat color her cheeks. "I'm sorry."

"No need to apologize. No one likes to wait on a long line if they have something better to do." Jake's smile hinted he would have done the same thing.

Lilliana had hooked her finger in Les's collar as he edged his way out of the room. "Like a thief, trying to sneak away."

"Enjoy the show, Morgan?" Jake asked.

Les stopped in his tracks. "Fleichman, what are you doing here? Going to buy the dance school for your little girl like you bought the bakery for your family?"

"No such luck, Morgan. I wouldn't take this run-down building off your hands that easily." Jake peeled a speck of paint off the wall. "Actually I heard the gossip circulating out front."

Little beads of sweat dampened Les's forehead. "This is none of your concern, Fleichman."

"What's the matter, Morgan, afraid I caught you at your own game?" Jake turned to Rebecca. "Did he offer you time to work out Lilliana's problem?"

Rebecca nodded.

"It's probably in the lease. He can't just throw Lilliana out. Old man Morgan anticipated he wouldn't be around forever. He raised Les to be a businessman. Les inherited his father's business but not his instinct for compassion. The old man knew there might be problems."

"He was a mensch your father, a decent person. Not like you." Lilliana poked her finger in Les's chest.

"Listen, Fleichman, we go way back." Les placed his arm over Jake's shoulder. "I know we had a little misunderstanding over the bakery. If you have to, you'll find your daughter another dance school."

Rebecca watched Jake. She was trained to be aware of how those around her moved. Both men were the same height but that was where the similarity ended. Les was thin all the way down to his toes while Jake had broad shoulders that tapered down to a narrow waist.

Jake leaned casually against the wall with his arms crossed over his chest. "We like the school in this building." He seemed to be enjoying this confrontation with Les.

"Jake Fleichman, everybody's hero." Les parted the curtain. "I'm not hanging around while you charm these ladies into believing your offer comes solely from your heart."

"A heart is something you would know nothing about," Lilliana said as she held the curtain open, encouraging Les to leave.

Before passing through, Les looked at Rebecca. "My offer is sincere. I have nothing to lose. If you're smart you'll find out what Fleichman has to gain by helping you." The heavy drapes clapped together as he disappeared into its folds. The dense fabric rippled as Les's tall lanky form searched for an exit.

The sight of Les fighting to free himself from the velvet monster brought some levity to the whole situation. Lilliana's laughter was contagious.

Jake looked at Rebecca and then burst out laughing. "Should we help him?"

"Absolutely. I don't want his mood to become any worse."

They each reached for an end of the curtain and pulled them aside.

"Are you okay, Les?" Rebecca picked some lint off of his sleeve.

He brushed her hand away. "I'm being more than generous. Just watch out for this guy," Les said before he disappeared.

"What a miserable man." Lilliana grinned from ear to ear, then turned to Jake. "Where do you want to start?"

"Do you have any bills and receipts I could see?"

"I'll get my files."

"Maybe I should help you." Rebecca knew Lilliana's filing system consisted of some overstuffed old toeshoe boxes.

"No, no, you two wait here." Lilliana too disappeared into the folds of the curtain.

Rebecca felt a twinge of pain in her calf. A stream of water flowed on the uneven floor. She tried to step around the melted ice but misjudged her distance.

"Watch your step," Jake warned.

It was too late. Rebecca grasped at the air in an attempt to steady herself.

Jake had maneuvered behind her and almost as if it were a choreographed move, he slipped his arm around her waist. Jake found himself looking down into eyes as dark as black satin. He held her a little longer than necessary. Maybe his grandmother and Vinnie were right—it had been too long since he held a woman in his arms. He felt an empty ache when she moved away.

Jake's eyes roamed over her leotard-clad body. "You appear much taller on stage."

"Have you seen many ballets?" Rebecca reached for her T-shirt. She slipped the oversized shirt over her head, covering herself to her knees.

"Does this recital count?" He exchanged a smile with her, then shook his head. "Don't know a tutu from a slipper."

Rebecca smiled. "You're not alone. Most fathers have little interest in their daughters' dance classes."

Jake watched Rebecca walk to the sink. Her movements and attitude reflected the agility and aloofness of a cat. "Actually it was my grandmother who signed her up. I don't think I could raise Jewel without her."

"Oh." She gathered a handful of towels and bent down to wipe up the spill. He couldn't help noticing she didn't bear all her weight on her right leg.

Jake got down on his hands and knees, facing her. "Did you hurt your leg?"

"It's an occupational hazard." Her tone suggested she didn't want to talk about it.

Rising, Jake offered his hand. Rebecca reached up and accepted it. With gentle pressure he helped her to her feet.

"Les doesn't like you very much, does he?" she asked.

"We've had our differences." Jake's eyes moved from the top of Rebecca's twisted plaits to the end of her leg warmers. He hadn't realized how warm it was backstage. "Doesn't the air work?"

"Just one of the many things wrong with this building."

The kind of heat Jake was feeling had nothing to do with the temperature.

She stood facing him. "Does Lilliana know you're not very knowledgeable about the ballet?"

Jake could tell she was trying to choose her words carefully. "I'm completely ignorant about ballet." He shrugged. "I don't think she cares."

"I'm sure your intentions are sincere, but you probably don't understand the scope of the problem." Rebecca tossed the saturated towels into the trash can and extended her hand to Jake. "I'll tell her you didn't realize how difficult this was going to be." She walked across the room and picked up her leather satchel. With her back to him, she started to pack her equipment.

"She won't believe I didn't know what I was getting into. I know this neighborhood and the people who do business here." Jake followed her. "A business is a business." He tried to keep the sarcasm out of his voice. "Ballet schools, bakeries, or restaurants, they all work on the same principle. You have to bring in more than you spend."

"Comparing food and dance is like comparing apples and oranges," Rebecca chided.

"Don't dancers eat?" He liked the way her hair sat in tight plaits around her head. It heightened the sensual length of her neck.

"I wish you'd stay focused." She squared her shoulders, accentuating her neck. She looked directly at him. "Of course we eat. If you're serious about helping Lilliana, we need to discuss her problem and not food."

"I'm very serious about helping Lilliana." Her gracious but haughty attitude made him smile.

"Yoo-hoo," a shrill voice called from the stage. "Anyone back there?"

Jake stepped forward to assist a stout old lady through the folds of heavy curtain.

"Hello, Sadie." Rebecca smiled at the woman who had been making costumes for Lilliana's recitals for decades. "Are you looking for Lil?"

"No, actually I want to speak to you." She picked a long white thread off her skirt. "I heard Lil was having some problems. I didn't want to bother her."

"Are the costumes paid for?" Rebecca asked.

"Well, yes and no." Sadie shook her head from side to side.

"How much does she owe you?"

"Just for the final alterations. Twenty dollars, a dollar more or less."

Rebecca reached into her bag. She fumbled with the contents before finding her checkbook.

"What do you carry in there? The Empire State Building?" Sadie peeked into the bag.

"Just about." Rebecca smiled. "If I write a check for thirty dollars, will that cover it?"

"Thirty's good." Sadie studied the check for a moment, folded it, and tucked it into her ample bosom. Before she left she winked at Jake and said, "She's got a good head on her shoulders." She smiled at Rebecca. "And a pretty one."

"Sadie's a sweetheart. A wizard with a needle and thread," Rebecca said. "Her costumes can make any little girl feel like a princess."

Jake tried to picture Rebecca at Jewel's age, all puffed up in a pink tutu. Hard as he tried, he couldn't remember ever having seen her before. "You grow up around here?" he asked.

"Not far from here," she said. "Why?"

"It's just that I've never seen you before."

"I don't live here any more." She tilted her chin and looked directly at him. "I haven't lived here for years."

Rebecca Carr might be a little uppity but she had an unbelievably sexy neck. He had to remain focused if she was to believe he really wanted to help Lilliana.

"Have you been writing personal checks to cover Lilliana's debts?" Jake asked.

"This is the first time."

"Don't let word get out, or you'll have a line of creditors at your door."

Rebecca chewed on her lower lip and looked at him. "I didn't realize."

As if conjured up by his warning, a gruff voice called out. "Hey, back there. The dance teacher there?"

"I'm a teacher." Rebecca's T-shirt was so large it began to slip off her shoulder.

"Let me handle this," Jake said.

"Hey, Fleichman, whatcha doing back here?" The cigar hanging from the man's pudgy lips jiggled with each word. "My boss said to make sure I spoke to the old lady in charge." He glared at Rebecca's bare shoulder. "But you'll do."

Jake covered Rebecca's shoulder with the oversized shirt, then stepped in front of her. Once she was safe from the man's lewd glare, he asked, "What can I do for you, Pete?"

"I came to pick up the rented chairs, but the boss warned me I better not leave without a check. I can't seem to find the old lady who runs the place."

"How much does she owe you?" Rebecca peeked over Jake's shoulder.

"A c-note."

"How much?" Rebecca repeated.

Pete handed the bill to Jake. "It's all there. Cost of the chair rental, pick up, and delivery."

"One hundred dollars? For how many chairs?" Jake held the bill up to Pete's face.

"Fifty chairs. It says so right there."

"That's absurd."

"I'm only pickin' up. You gotta problem, speak to the boss." He turned to leave. "I'll go find the old lady. It's her bill."

Rebecca stepped in front of Jake. Before he could intervene she had her check book and pen in her hand. "I'll take care of the bill. I'm sure there's no need to bother Lilliana."

"Thanks, sweetheart. You just made my job easier." The man nodded in Jake's direction. "See ya around, Fleichman."

"You shouldn't have paid him so fast." Jake tried not to let the anger come through in his voice. "I know this neighborhood and the merchants. I could have worked something out."

"I don't see what the big deal is. Lilliana owed him money and now she doesn't."

"Writing personal checks will not get Lilliana out of this mess. It won't take long for word to spread. I'm afraid you may have already opened Pandora's box." His words were a little harsher than he wanted them to be. "If we're going to be working together, you better let me deal with any creditors."

"I don't recall agreeing to work with you." Rebecca chided in her defense.

"We do agree Lilliana needs help." He looked around the deserted room. "I don't see anyone else offering."

"You are the best offer we've gotten all day, but I don't understand why you're doing this." He could hear the uncertainty in her voice. "Why don't you go over the files before we make any decisions. You might change your mind."

Maybe she was just being cautious. He could understand her hesitation. After all, he was a perfect stranger to her. "You're right. I'll look over the files and then we'll have something to discuss. Are you free Monday?"

Rebecca didn't answer immediately. "Tomorrow? You expect to have gone through all of her receipts in one day?"

"It will give me a rough idea of what needs to be done,"

Fox Lake District Library

Jake said. "We can meet at the Bridge Cafe tomorrow evening."

"I'd have to come back to Brooklyn again," Rebecca said.

"You don't like coming here?"

"During the ballet season my schedule is very busy. I hardly ever leave the city." She looked down at her leg. A haunted look clouded her eyes. "Unfortunately I've recently found myself with an unwanted vacation. The season is over and my troupe is touring Europe."

"We'll have to find a reason for you to come more often, now that you have so much free time." Jake knew he was getting close to her feelings, so he tried to lighten the conversation. He wasn't ready to share any of his feelings in return.

"My injury only limits my classes. I'm still busy with physical therapy appointments and workouts."

"Are you free tomorrow evening?" He waited for her response. "Don't worry about reservations. I have a personal connection."

"Okay, the Bridge Cafe tomorrow evening." Rebecca smiled.

"Then it's safe to say we have a date tomorrow about eight," Jake said.

"Eight is fine, but let's not refer to our meeting as a date." Her voice held a note of concern. "I'd like to keep our association strictly business."

"Whatever you say." The thought of seeing her again felt good, but Jake wasn't anxious to rush into an intimate relationship no matter how attractive the offering.

Lilliana came in balancing a stack of boxes. "Here are the bills and recital costs you asked to see."

Behind her followed a gaggle of little ballerinas. Their

almost-buns stuck together with tons of hair spray. One of the girls rushed over to Jake. "Hi, Miss Becky. Hi, Dad. I see you two finally met. Miss Lilliana said you might need some help."

"I think we're going to need all the help we can get." Jake glanced sideways at Rebecca. "I'm going to need someone who understands all those fancy French words." He winked at Jewel.

Jewel giggled. "My dad doesn't even know what a leotard is. He needs lots of help."

Jake wanted to correct Jewel. He knew very well what a leotard was and how sensational Rebecca Carr looked in her body suit and tights. An image focused in his memory: he envisioned her elegant form twirling on stage. Chiffon and lace flowed over her perfect body.

Rebecca smiled at Jewel. "I hope his business knowledge is more adequate."

"Don't worry, Dad's a financial whiz." Jewel began to speak but stopped when Jake gave her a firm parental glare.

"Let's not bore Miss Becky with unnecessary stuff," he said.

"Whatever you say, Dad."

Jake turned to Rebecca and said, "You know how kids are, always saying their parents are the best." He extended his hand to Rebecca. "So it's a deal."

Rebecca hesitated before accepting his hand. Jake followed her eyes as they stopped on each person in the room. Lilliana bent over her boxes trying to sort out canceled checks and receipts. Jewel stood between them, studying first her father then Rebecca. Rebecca's eyes searched his face. Pride and uncertainty mingled in her glance.

With his hand still extended, he waited. His eyes challenged her to accept his offer.

"Yes, but strictly business," she said firmly.

"Absolutely, strictly business." Jake imitated her serious tone. I'll call you to confirm our meeting." Jake condensed Lilliana's files. He gave Jewel a light load to carry and balanced the remaining boxes under his chin. At his signal Jewel followed with her stash. He would honor Rebecca's request to keep their association a business one. She had already managed to stir feelings he had not allowed to surface in years.

Chapter Three

J ake ran his fingers through his hair. Lilliana's finances were in a worse state than he could have ever imagined. Her checks bounced around her like ballerinas. Bankruptcy loomed in the wings. Her final recital had cost more to stage than she sold in tickets. The further he looked, the worse it got.

The firm knock on his office door brought a welcome relief from the mess of bills and receipts scattered across his desk.

"Come in," Jake encouraged the intruder.

"There ya are, boss." Vinnie scanned the chaos. "What's all this?"

"I offered to help Lilliana sort through some financial problems."

"Ya did?" Vinnie picked up some bills, glanced at them

and tossed them back onto the desk. "What's a matter with ya, don't ya have enough to do?"

"Look at this mess. The poor woman has no idea how to manage a business." Jake waved his hand across a stack of checks, accidentally knocking several onto the floor.

Vinnie glanced at the back of the checks. "These were never cashed."

"Exactly. There are several generous checks that were never cashed." Jake glanced at his watch. "Help is on the way. I'm expecting one of the instructors from the Academy. I hope she can explain why so many students are behind in their tuition."

"Ya don't mean the sexy broad who came into the bakery the other day?" Vinnie flashed a wide grin.

Jake placed his hands on his old friend's shoulders. "What was it you wanted when you came in?"

"I get it. I won't ask about her again. One of the sous chefs is ready to kill himself over his new sauce."

"Then I better go see what I can do to help."

The two men walked side by side into the main dining room. Before they entered the swinging door to the kitchen, Vinnie stopped. He turned to Jake. "Hey, wait a minute. Doesn't that creep Les Morgan own the school building?"

"Not for much longer, if I can help it."

"So that's it. You're after Morgan again. What if he finds out? Ya know how he likes to stick a monkey wrench in and mess up your plans."

"By the time he finds out, he'll have a big fat check in his hand and Lilliana will be free of him. I'm not going to tell him. Are you?" A smile curved Jake's lips. "I think I've found a way to put a stop to his greed. He can't keep violating his tenants' rights, especially the older ones.

They've worked too hard to lose their businesses to someone like Morgan."

"You're not going to buy that run-down old building for Lilliana, like you did for your grandparents."

"That would be a financial disaster. I've got other plans this time." Jake pushed the door open. "Do me a favor and wait out here for the ballerina."

"Ya got it, boss."

The street lights above the trees flashed on as Rebecca stepped from the taxi. She looked at the surrounding area. Amid a row of neat, well-preserved Federal houses sat the Bridge Cafe.

Rebecca had decided to do some research of her own before she met Jake. It wasn't hard to find information about the Bridge Cafe. It had received rave reviews from every food critic in New York. The one thing Mr. Fleichman had failed to tell her was the most impressive. Jake Fleichman was executive chef/owner of the famous restaurant.

"Welcome." Vinnie greeted her as she entered.

Rebecca looked around the empty restaurant. "I'm here to meet Mr. Fleichman." She extended her hand to Vinnie. "Rebecca Carr."

"Nice to meet ya. I'm Vinnie. I manage the joint." Vinnie grasped her hand firmly. "The boss'll be right with ya. He's in the kitchen. Some problem with a maple citrus glaze one of the sous chefs is experimenting with."

Rebecca looked around. The dining room was empty. "No customers tonight?"

"We're closed on Mondays," Vinnie said. "The kitchen crew likes to come in and experiment with new dishes."

With a loud bang the double doors from the kitchen flew

open. "I'll never get the consistency. I don't know how Jake does it." A stout young man stopped short when he saw Rebecca. "So you're the ballerina. Nice, very nice. The boss will be right with you. He's trying to make a sauce out of the mess I made." Before he went back into the kitchen he spoke to Vinnie. Together they glanced at Rebecca and nodded.

"The chef wants to know what you'd like to eat." Vinnie regarded her with amusement. "Thinks you're too skinny."

First the ladies in the bakery and now this chef. If everyone Jake knew tried to offer her food, she would never be in shape when the ballet season started. "No thanks. I've already had dinner."

The chef shrugged and walked back into the kitchen. Through the little window Rebecca noticed his cherub face pressed against the round glass. He waited for his cue to perform.

Rebecca smiled at him. He smiled back, his eyes disappearing in the creases of his face. "Maybe some coffee," she said.

"And a dessert," Vinnie encouraged her.

"Oh no. No dessert."

"We specialize in light. Low-fat and chic, the secret of our success." Vinnie winked at her. "Leave it to me. Have a seat. I'll see what's keepin' the boss."

Rebecca walked over to the bar. She pulled herself up onto one of the elaborately cushioned stools. Behind her a warm, country French decor gave the dining room an elegant air. She was surprised how many of her associates had dined at the Bridge Cafe. From stagehands to dancers on the line, the well-known restaurant and its owner received rave reviews. Rebecca wondered why Jake had failed to mention that he owned the place.

Through the reflection in the bar mirror Rebecca saw Jake emerge through the swinging doors. What had possessed her to agree to this meeting?

She was surprised to see him dressed in a chef's tunic. The top of the tunic hung loose and flapped against his muscular chest. He approached with caution, balancing a plate of fresh berries and two steaming cups of coffee. The man looked just as attractive as he did in a bakery apron.

"Hi. Glad you made it."

Rebecca hopped off the stool and walked over to greet him. "I hate to admit it but my curiosity got the better of me. I wanted to see for myself why a reservation here is so hard to get." She glanced around the dimly lit dining room. "So you own this place." She sighed. "And I thought you worked in—" she started.

"It's nothing, just a local neighborhood place." Jake could not suppress his laugh.

"What's so funny?"

"What did you think I had in mind? A bake sale? You don't realize how transparent you are." Jake placed the plate and cups on the bar. He got down on his knees and clasped his hand to his chest. "*Your face, my thane, is as a book where men may read strange matters.*"

"Get off your knees." She looked at him, eyes widening. "This is no time to quote Shakespeare."

"Ah, you recognized Lady Macbeth's warning to her husband." Jake stood up. He took a step toward her. "Even now I can read the surprise in your face. I like honesty in women, however they express it."

"And what am I thinking?" She lifted her chin and met his gaze straight on.

"This Brooklyn boy who knows nothing about ballet can recite Shakespeare." He waited for her to come back at him with a smart remark. She didn't. "How would old Will have said you can take the boy out of Brooklyn but you can't take Brooklyn out of the boy?"

"You have no idea what I was thinking." She snapped her mouth shut.

"I know exactly what you're thinking." He lowered his gaze and looked at her suspiciously. "You thought I was stuck in the old neighborhood. Stuck behind the counter in my grandparents' bakery."

"You never said you owned one of the most successful restaurants in New York."

"Would that have made a difference? My offer to help Lilliana is sincere."

Rebecca didn't need to answer. It was written all over her face. When he first noticed her in the bakery, he could tell she felt uncomfortable. Maybe dancers were like that. You could read their emotions in every move.

"You doubt the sincerity of my offer."

"I just don't understand why you would go through all this trouble to help an old lady save her school."

Jake hadn't planned on explaining his reasons. But he thought now that they were to have a working relationship, it was probably for the best that she understand some of his motives. At least the ones he wanted to share. He didn't know her well enough to be completely open.

"I owe everything I have to the education I got on the streets of the old neighborhood." He waved his hands in the air. "So do you, in a way."

"I don't disagree. I am who I am because Lilliana developed my gift."

"Now wasn't that easy—we're both doing this to help Lilliana." He studied her face, feature by feature, and watched her mask of uncertainty fade. "I've gone through that mess Lilliana calls her files. I have to admit there's a lot I don't understand."

"Maybe I can explain some of them."

"Let's get started." Jake picked up the plates.

He didn't look directly at Rebecca; instead he watched her reflection in the mirror. Her hair was twisted into a tight bun. He wondered if she ever wore it loose. An air of romantic elegance surrounded her. He handed her the plate of berries.

Rebecca walked in the direction of the empty dining room.

"I thought we'd work in my office, but if you'd rather sit out here I can gather up the papers I've put together."

"Oh no, your office will be fine." She hesitated before she took the plate. "I really don't have to eat this if you don't allow food in your office."

"This is a restaurant. We allow food any place the law permits." Jake nodded toward the kitchen. Vinnie had joined the chef at the tiny round window. "They'll be very insulted if you refuse their offering."

With her plate in hand Rebecca followed. Inside the office Rebecca was drawn to the back wall. Shelves of cookbooks ran the length of the room.

"You've got some collection." She ran her finger across the bindings. She paused for a moment to read the titles. "I never realized there was so much to say about food."

"Feel free to browse while I make some sense of this mess." Jake looked up at the sound of a book closing. "What kind of foods do you like?" His books were arranged by regions, ingredients, and courses. He knew exactly which book Rebecca had slipped back onto the shelf: *Romantic French Meals*. "Do you like French food?"

"Not particularly." Rebecca looked over her shoulder. "Have you ever done a TV cooking show?"

"There's a guy from the network who asked me to do a spot," Jake said.

"Why don't you do it?" Rebecca asked.

"I'm looking for the right gimmick."

"You mean a bam here and a bam there." Rebecca said.

"Exactly, but that's been done." Jake was surprised she knew anything about the Food Network. "Have you ever done a TV show?"

"A very short segment," she said. "I was once the B for Ballerina on Sesame Street."

"No kidding." Jake couldn't hide his smile.

Rebecca gave a lofty laugh. "Why would I lie about something like that."

In spite of her grand attitude Jake found her enchanting. He pulled out a chair for her. "Better taste your dessert before it gets too soggy."

Jake watched her shuffle the berries across the plate. She pierced a fat juicy raspberry and slowly put it in her mouth. The juice stained her already red lips. She licked her lower lip and then dabbed it with the napkin. He forced himself to look away.

"Mmm, it's very fresh."

"We use the best. Our customers would never accept less." Jake could talk about food forever. "What do you cook?"

"I don't." Rebecca shrugged. "I eat on the run. Mostly salads and yogurt."

"Do you ever eat anything that's not good for you?"

"Like what?" Rebecca looked puzzled by his question.

"Cake, ice cream, some of the simple pleasures of life."

"Not worth the extra calories."

Jake hid his smile. She was serious. Food did not sit high on her list. She ate to fuel her well-maintained body. A very well-maintained body.

Jeans covered Rebecca's strong dancer's legs. Under her blouse he caught a glimpse of black lace and his eyes immediately followed the curve of her neck. He would love to teach her the finer points of eating. He savored the thought of her tantalized taste buds responding to the flavor and textures of his signature dishes.

He took a sip of coffee: hot, black, no sugar. The bitter taste helped him regroup his thoughts. Business, not pleasure, he reminded himself. "We've got a lot to discuss. Let's get to it."

"Good idea." Rebecca lifted her fork and pointed it at Jake. "Now that you've gone through Lilliana's hodge-podge bookkeeping, do you still think you can help?"

"I didn't have to look through too much to see the school is in desperate need of financial reorganization." He waited for her response. Like an elegant statue she sat perfectly still, so he continued. "I'll have to start with the creditors' calls."

"How do you expect to pay off these creditors?" She looked at him with her big chocolate eyes. "The problem is, Lilliana doesn't have the money."

"I ruled out a bake sale when I saw the scope of her debt." Seeing the amusement in her eyes, he laughed.

Leaning forward and resting her chin on her hand, Rebecca had a thoughtful smile on her lips. "I'm listening. Explain your plan."

"Actually I have several ideas. First Morgan needs to be paid off."

At the mention of Morgan's name, Rebecca bolted upright. "Les's bark is worse than his bite. I happen to know the school was in trouble before he entered the picture. I just didn't realize how deep. Lilliana doesn't think about money."

"Everyone thinks about money." It bothered Jake that Rebecca seemed to jump to Morgan's defense.

"Not Lilliana. She's an artist." Rebecca reached for another berry. Her lips puckered. Jake hoped a tart berry caused her sour expression and not his comment.

"I told her you wouldn't understand," Rebecca said.

"That's why she insisted I let you help."

"You mean you were going to do this on your own?" This time there was no question Rebecca's lips puckered with uneasiness. "Did you just walk up to Lilliana and offer to help?"

"In a way." Jake nodded. "Lilliana said she had someone who might be interested in my plan." He purposely left out some details. He had been talking to Lilliana, asking about the young lady who came into the bakery. Some of the parents approached with offers to raise money. Although their offers were sincere they were amateurs. They would run bake sales and car washes and solicit local merchants. Jake had more influential resources.

He studied Rebecca's face. Her lips relaxed and she exhaled a long sigh. "Did you ask the parents to help you?" she asked.

"No. Now that I've gone through this mess, I realize Lilliana knew this was too much for those well-meaning people." He picked up some papers. "Can you explain these?"

Rebecca looked at the uncashed checks. "That's easy."

"I'm listening." Jake crossed his hands behind his neck and leaned back.

"Susie and Rochelle Leigh were generous backers of the

school for many years. Not too long ago they pulled their support."

"Why didn't Lilliana cash their checks?"

"Most likely Lilliana thought they were pulling out because they had personal financial problems," Rebecca offered.

"Are the checks good?" Jake asked.

"Of course they are. Unfortunately the old girls had promised money to too many charities. Lilliana's school came up on their drop list."

"If these were written in good faith, she should cash them." Jake put the checks in an envelope and handed it to Rebecca.

"I'll see that Lilliana gets them." Rebecca rested her elbows on the desk. "Tell me your next step."

"A fund raiser." He watched the swell of her breasts rising and falling over the lace trim of her camisole. "I'll use the restaurant as the drawing point."

"Sounds like a good idea."

Jake walked behind her chair. "Want to see the guest list?" He reached over her shoulder and handed her a paper napkin with names scribbled on it. His face brushed close to her hair. A mix of orange blossoms, jasmine, and lavender captured his senses.

"Is there Neroli oil in your shampoo?" He inhaled her essence.

She didn't pull away. "It's possible. I buy a special citrus blend. It's made in a little boutique on Lexington Avenue."

"Did you know the oil comes from the orange blossom? We sometimes use it in cooking. But it always reminds me of a folk tale."

Rebecca cupped her plaited bun. "A folk tale?" She turned to face him.

"It's just a tale about a newlywed couple. The groom had orange blossoms added to the bridal bouquet. He believed the scent would have a calming effect on his bride before they retired for the evening." He was pleased by her interest. She watched him intently waiting for the climax. "You know the rest," he said.

"Like a tale from a classical ballet." Rebecca sighed. "They lived happily ever after."

"You believe in happily ever after?" Jake pulled a chair next to her's. She radiated a charm that drew him.

"Don't you?" she asked, her eyes wide open.

"Not anymore." Jake reminded himself they were not here tonight to discuss alluring scents or fairy tale endings. "We've got work to do." Looking over her shoulder, he pointed out some of the high-profile names on his list.

It didn't take long for them to get back on track. "It reads like a Who's Who of New York," she said, her eyes following his finger. "The Mayor of New York?"

"He's a frequent diner. I also think he'll be a big help in the second step."

"What's the second step?" She asked.

"Unless we can convince Lilliana to relocate, we'll have to find a way to renovate the building."

"Never. She'd never leave that old building. Everything about it fits like a well-worn toeshoe." Rebecca sighed. "I tried to convince her years ago to move to the city and set up a school."

"She's just like my grandparents. They rather see the roof cave in on their heads." Jake shrugged. "They're a tough old breed. Raising money to pay off the creditors is the easy part. We still have an old building to deal with."

"I don't know anything about construction, but I imagine

it's going to take a lot of money to fix that old building."
She listened, interested in what he had to say.

"The price of a ticket to the affair should cover most of
Lilliana's debt." Jake took the napkin from her. "We'll
need help with permits and plans." He pointed to the
Mayor's name. "Might as well start with the man at the
top."

"You seem to know what you're doing." Rebecca smiled.
"You've done your homework. I recognize most of the
names on this list. Some are already generous benefactors
of the City Ballet." She shook her head. "Will they support
a small Brooklyn ballet school?"

Jake tried hard to ignore the skeptical sound of her voice.

"I'm still not sure why you're doing this?" she asked.

"I'm a sucker for lost causes." Jake gave her a teasing
smile. "You don't believe that, do you?"

"You don't even like the ballet. And Les said it best—
there are other schools for your daughter."

"What do you think?" Jake asked. "Why am I doing this?
Surely I have enough to keep me busy. Raising my daugh-
ter is full-time work. I may not cut the meat anymore, but
I still have recipes to test and a five-star restaurant to run."

"It's obvious you don't need the publicity." She gestured
at the list.

"Not worth the effort. Serve good food and word of
mouth is the best publicity there is. People want to talk
about a restaurant when they leave." His lips curled in the
start of a laugh. "A recent listing in *Zagat's* helped too."

"I like your optimistic attitude." The skepticism hadn't
vanished from her voice. "I hope you can convince your
guests this is a worthy cause."

"Our guests. Remember we're working together on this.
Anyone you would like to add?"

"There are two names I would add."

"Who?" Jake asked.

"Dave Burke is one." She waited for the name to register. "Do you know him?"

"Everyone knows the Iron Man of Wall Street."

"Does he dine here too?" she asked.

"He used to. I heard he hasn't been out socially since his wife died."

"He'll come for Lilliana. They're old friends."

"Talk about fattening up for the kill, why didn't she just ask him for help? He's one of the most benevolent men in New York."

"Lilliana would never take advantage of their friendship," Rebecca explained.

"So how does the old girl know Mr. Wall Street?"

Rebecca smiled. "Dave and Lilliana go way back. They were friends when she danced with the City Ballet. Actually, rumor has it they were more than friends, but Lilliana wasn't ready to give up dancing."

Jake wondered if all dancers found it hard to choose marriage over their careers. He never thought of Lilliana as a career woman. He knew all about women on the fast track. He had been married to one. "Did Lilliana let him go so she could continue her dance career?"

"Not exactly. She introduced him to a costume designer. They fell in love and were married for over fifty years. The Burkes have always been big supporters of the ballet."

"Who would have thought. Mr. Wall Street at the ballet. I always thought Dave was more the Yankee Stadium type."

"He is. Has a box behind home plate."

"You've been to a game with him?" Jake couldn't keep

the surprise out of his voice. "You like baseball? You may not be as predictable as I thought."

Rebecca clasped her hand to her heart. *"Your face, my thane, is as a book where men may read strange matters."*

"Touché." Jake laughed. He found it difficult to refrain from asking Rebecca questions about her personal life. "I didn't realize ballerinas liked anything except the ballet."

"With classes, practice, rehearsals, we don't have much time for anything else."

"Any other power magnets I forgot?" Jake asked.

Rebecca hesitated. "Just one. He's kind of powerful in his own way."

"I don't think you can top the last name you added."

"In a way I might." She chewed on her lip.

"I'm waiting." He put up his hands as if ready to catch a fast ball. "Hit me with it."

"I think we should invite Les."

Jake grabbed a handful of bounced checks and crushed them in a closed fist. "Did you forget he's the one responsible for this mess?"

"I was afraid you would react this way." Rebecca took the papers and attempted to smooth out the wrinkles. "Why can't the two of you get along?"

"What makes you think we don't get along?" He waited for her to comment. She didn't. "My reasons are personal."

She smiled. "I know we agreed not to go there."

"Business only. I'm trying to comply with your rules." It was a good rule. Jake had decided a long time ago not to share his private affairs with new acquaintances, especially beautiful women. As attractive as she was, she would pass out of his life as quickly as she had entered. He reminded himself they would never see each other again after the fund raiser.

"You're a man of your word." Rebecca touched his arm. "I also happen to know Lilliana was in financial trouble before Les added to her problems."

Her closeness disturbed him. He stepped behind his desk. "It's no secret the woman is not a financial wiz."

Rebecca followed Jake. She stood right beside him and opened Lilliana's impromptu ledger.

"See these listings?" As she turned the pages, her arm brushed against his. It gave him an unexpected sensation.

Jake focused on the names she pointed to. "Cindy, Myra, Tanya." He read out loud. "There are no last names, and each one owes several months' tuition."

"Those are some of Lilliana's more affluent students."

"So why are they behind in payment?" Jake asked.

"Lilliana is an artist. She molds dancers. She pays little attention to anything but her students."

Jake sat down in his chair. "Are you trying to justify Lilliana's imperfections or Morgan's flaws?"

"If your party raises enough money to pay off Les and fix up the building, everything will be perfect and no one will be at fault."

Could she be baiting him? Her simple explanation and soft manner made his hostile feeling toward Morgan seem trivial. "Why is Morgan's presence so important?"

Without hesitation, Rebecca answered. "He could point out major structural problems to the Mayor."

"Good try. But no cigar. You don't need to be Frank Lloyd Wright to see the building is in need of repair."

A short silence, then Rebecca whispered. "He could. . . ." She shifted in her seat and struggled to find another reason.

Everything was going so well, Jake didn't want her to suddenly become uncomfortable. "Okay, it's your party too. I'll see that he gets a formal invitation."

"I'm sure he'll be pleased." He liked the way her face brightened.

"He pays for a plate just like the other guests," Jake added.

"Absolutely." Rebecca smiled.

"And the affair is black tie. He goes for the cost of a tux just like everyone else."

"No problem. I know Les owns a tuxedo. I've seen him wear it to the opening of the ballet."

"Morgan at the ballet," he repeated. "Who would have thought Les Morgan at the ballet."

"He's a season ticket holder." Rebecca stifled a laugh. His reaction seemed to amuse her. "Have you ever been to the ballet?"

"I'd rather have an earache." As soon as the words were out, Jake regretted his comment. "It just seems so confusing. All that jumping and spinning. No one speaking."

"I understand. You'd be bored."

Seeing the amusement in her eyes, he laughed. "I guess you got me on that one. How about a quick synopsis of the ballet?"

"It might be easier to teach me how to cook."

"I'm sure you'll do fine. I've been told you're one of Lilliana's most famous students. A prima ballerina."

Rebecca blushed. "Who told you that?"

"My daughter, my grandmother, some old ladies in the bakery. Remember, I'm the guy who can't tell a tutu from a slipper. What's a prima ballerina?"

"A principal dancer who dances the leads. Sort of like the executive chef."

Stretching his arms, Jake leaned back and rested his head in clasped hands. He could focus all his attention on her sensuous lips, alluring dark eyes, and sexy neck. She was warm and enchanting when she spoke about the ballet. He didn't want her to stop.

"There are soloists and the corps de ballet who perform together as fairies, swans, and so on."

"It must be hard work."

"That's our job to make it all come together and look easy." She rubbed her leg as she spoke.

"And the show must go on." Jake nodded in the direction of her injury.

Rebecca pulled her hand away. "Dance becomes your life. I can't imagine what Lilliana would do if she loses the school."

"What would you do if you couldn't dance?"

"There's nothing else I could imagine doing." There was a slight quiver in her voice.

He noticed her uneasiness. Did she see her own vulnerability in the school's problems?

Rebecca stood and walked toward the door. "Enough about me. I've never been backstage in a restaurant. How about a tour?"

"It all starts right here." Jake pounded his chest. "There's me, the chef."

"I know, Jake Fleichman, Executive Chef/Owner."

"You've done some checking too."

"I wanted to know in whose hands we're placing the future of Lilliana's Dance Academy."

"I'll introduce you to some of the swans and fairies who help put this show on the road." She didn't object when he placed his arm around her waist and guided her through the door. All business partners should feel this soft and inviting. Too enticing. He released his hold.

*   *   *

Smooth white tiles and unblemished stainless steel lined the walls and floors of the kitchen.

It appeared the sous chef had been successful. His sausage-fingered hand gave the sauce a final stir. "You're just in time to deliver a verdict." The spoon he handed to Jake dripped with savory thick orange glaze.

Jake twisted the spoon catching every drop of citrus sauce. He let the combination of scents fill his nostrils. Then he placed a small dab on the tip of his tongue. He savored the delicate union of sweet sticky maple syrup and tart citrus. Satisfied with the smooth texture and perfect blend, he allowed the sauce to glide down his throat.

Jake responded first with a nod, then a smile, and finally with a hearty clap on the chef's back. "You've got it."

The sous chef's pudgy face melted into a buttery smile. He gave the sauce one more stir and reached for a clean spoon. He dipped it in the pan and insisted Rebecca try his successful concoction. Her smile was all the reward he needed.

Vinnie grabbed the man's chubby cheeks and pinched each one. "You did it. We knew you'd get it."

The waiters all nodded in agreement.

In turn the sous chef placed his hands on Rebecca's face and kissed first her right then her left cheek. "You are my good-luck charm. I will name the sauce after you. It will become my signature recipe." He pressed his fingers to his lips and blew a kiss of approval in the air. "Okay with you, boss?"

"It's your sauce." Jake stood off to the side. He watched as the little chef took Rebecca's hands and danced her around the kitchen in tiny victory circles. She looked so gracious and regal as they twirled between the stainless steel counters.

Vinnie nudged Jake with his elbow. "Join in the celebration."

"I'll pass." Jake wondered what it would be like to take her in his arms, hold her close, and dance to the slow beat of an alluring melody. He wasn't a bad dancer. She might be impressed.

Exhausted, with beads of sweat on his forehead, the portly chef swung Rebecca to a stop in front of Jake. "Your turn, boss."

Rebecca already stood close and yet she managed to ease herself forward with her hands extended.

Jake put up his hands to form a barrier. He refused her offer. Taking a step back, he leaned against the shiny metal counter.

Rebecca stroked the smooth edge of the counter. Her fingers inched close to Jake's. Too close. Jake pulled his hand away and stepped around Rebecca. "I think things went well this evening. We accomplished more than I thought we would."

The sous chef picked up a cloth to wipe the prints off his clean counter. Vinnie grabbed the little man by the shoulder, and together they exited through the swinging doors.

"What's the next step?" Rebecca asked.

"I'll give you a call when the RSVPs start coming in." Jake held the door open. "Do you need a ride back?"

"You have things to do here. Don't bother, I can call a cab," she answered quickly.

"I was going to ask the crew if anyone was driving to the city."

As the color rose in Rebecca's cheeks, he realized she misunderstood. His question sounded like an offer to drive her home. He couldn't do that. He didn't want to be alone with her. She stirred too many emotions he had managed to keep hidden. "I'll have Vinnie call."

Jake's eyes were fixed on the yellow cab until it turned onto Montague Street. He would have sworn Rebecca was watching him too.

"How'd things go?" Vinnie asked. "Ya gonna save the school for the old lady?"

"I think our guests will be generous. They usually are. We should bring in enough money to pay off Lilliana's debts." Jake couldn't hide his annoyance.

"So what's troubling ya?"

"Morgan," Jake said.

"Les Morgan?" Vinnie repeated.

"Somehow I agreed to invite him."

"Ya what?" Vinnie's eyes opened wide. He was too surprised to speak.

"You heard me. Morgan's on the guest list."

"I know that wasn't your idea," Vinnie said.

"It was Rebecca's idea."

"Just like that." Vinnie threw his hands in the air. "You never let a pretty face cloud your judgment before."

"Her looks had nothing to do with it. We're partners in this affair. She had some good suggestions."

"Since when do you need help planning a party?"

"I don't." Jake put his arm around Vinnie's shoulder. "Maybe it's not such a big deal to invite him."

"No big deal?" Vinnie was shouting. "What were her reasons?"

"She didn't have a good reason and I couldn't think of one not to invite him."

"How about the man has been a thorn in your side and a menace to decent people."

"She doesn't see Morgan as such a monster." Jake

shrugged. "She's having a hard time believing my motives are unselfish."

"Are they?" Vinnie rubbed his chin. Jake knew that by his buddy's stance he was going to offer his advice. "Aside from getting in another shot at Morgan, do you have any hidden motives?" Vinnie asked. "You spent an awful long time in your office. She's got the look, ya know."

"What look?" Jake asked.

"The I'm available but I'm not sure if you're interested look."

"In two or three weeks this whole thing will be over, and we'll never see each other again."

"I don't believe ya. I saw the way ya looked at her when she was sitting at the bar. She didn't have the look when she came in. She looked unsure. Didn't want to be here. Whatever happened in your office must of changed her mind."

"Nothing happened." Jake crossed his arms on his chest and waited for Vinnie to finish. "She laid the ground rules. All business, no pleasure."

"Since when do you follow the rules?" Vinnie asked.

"I know where you're going with this." Since his divorce Jake had wedged a shield around his heart. Under the pretense of business, Rebecca had invaded his world. She treaded on sacred ground. First his grandparent's bakery, then a connection to his daughter, and now his restaurant. He wasn't ready to admit to himself or to Vinnie that she may have made a dent.

"You know what I think." Vinnie said.

"No, I don't want to know." Jake turned to walk back to the restaurant.

Vinnie was silent for a brief moment, then he laughed. "I'll tell you anyway. I think you like her. You like the way things went tonight and you're scared to death."

Chapter Four

Several days had passed and Rebecca hadn't heard from Jake. It was after eleven, but she was still awake doing the stretches recommended by her therapist. The phone rang.

Relieved to have a break from the tedious exercise, Rebecca reached for the phone. She held the receiver while she caught her breath. "Hello."

"Sorry to call you so late but you're a hard person to get in touch with," a deep sensual voice answered back.

"Jake Fleichman?" A short gasp escaped from the back of her throat.

"Yes," the male voice answered back. "If you've got someone there, I can call back anther time."

"No. I'm alone." She was stunned by the thrill of hearing his voice.

Rebecca rarely had visitors. Almost everyone she knew

was out of town touring with a dance company. Jake seemed to have friends everywhere he went. As she got older Rebecca worried because she knew so few people outside the ballet.

She sighed with regret. "Nobody here but me."

"Good. I wouldn't want to interrupt anything." He sounded a little too pleased to hear she was alone.

Rebecca felt a hot flush on her face. Jake's question had been suggestive. If he only knew there hadn't been anyone since her long-term relationship with a choreographer ended two years ago.

"How are the arrangements going?" she asked.

"Everything is fine. That's why I'm calling. I think we should meet with Lilliana. She might be interested in our progress."

"Good idea." Rebecca knew Lilliana would give her stamp of approval to anything Jake decided. She hated to admit it but she was eager to see him again. When she arrived at Jake's place the other evening, she had been prepared to leave if he showed any sign of a selfish motive behind his offer. The evening turned out to be more than she expected. Jake Fleichman was a very likable man.

Trying not to sound too enthusiastic, she waited a few seconds before continuing, "What's a good day for you?"

"How about tomorrow?"

"I've got a physical therapy appointment in the morning and then I'm free."

"I do the market in the morning so I'll be free around noon. Let's make it convenient for everyone. We'll do lunch at my grandparent's bakery."

"The Brooklyn bakery at noon." Rebecca never thought she would be spending so much time in Brooklyn. Working on the fund raiser with Jake Fleichman might be just the diversion she needed to take her mind off her unwanted vacation. "I'll be there."

"It's a date." Jake laughed as if sincerely amused. "Not a real date—it's just a figure of speech. See you tomorrow."

"Good night." Rebecca held the receiver against her breast. There was no buzz just silence on the other end. Jake hadn't hung up either.

She reached across her bed and placed the phone on its base.

"Some date," she whispered to herself. She ran down the list of chaperones: Lilliana, Jake's grandmother, and an assortment of Brooklyn yentas.

The phone rang again. Jumping across the bed, she picked up before the first ring ended. "Hi," she said in a suffocated whisper. "Calling back so soon. Did you forget to tell me something important?" Then she recognized the voice on the other end. "Oh, Les. Why are you calling so late?"

"It seems like I'm too late, as usual. Who did you think I was? I didn't think anyone you knew was still in the city."

"What do you want at this time of night?"

"I've been calling and leaving messages. How come you haven't called back? I thought we had an agreement. How did your meeting with Fleichman go?"

"It went fine. You should be getting an invitation soon."

"I got it today. Pretty hefty price your partner is asking for dinner at his place."

"You can afford it." She laughed to hide her annoyance. "The money goes to a worthy cause and it's tax deductible."

"It's like I'm betting against myself," Les said.

She remembered Jake saying something along those lines the other night. In so many ways Jake and Les were alike.

She couldn't understand the little war they were waging. "You don't have to come if you don't want to."

"And let Fleichman get one up on me? I'll be there."

"Great, see you at the party."

"I thought we could meet sooner and discuss the party plans."

"There's nothing to discuss."

"I just want to know what to expect. You could give me a rundown on the guests. I'm not far, I could stop by now. I just finished with a client at the Russian Tea Room."

"Les, I'm going to bed. It's eleven-forty five."

"Alone, I presume."

"Yes, alone." Suddenly everyone had an interest in her social life. "I've got a busy day tomorrow."

"With who? Wouldn't be the mystery man who called before me?"

"I never said it was a man."

"Are you saying it wasn't?" Les asked.

"I'm not saying anything."

"Okay, I guess our friendship doesn't give me the right to pry into your personal life."

"I don't have a personal life."

"You've seen Fleichman a couple of times."

He was baiting her now, trying to find out about the time she spent with Jake. "We've met to discuss the benefit."

"What are your plans for tomorrow?" Les asked.

"None of your business."

"Not like you to be so secretive. Maybe you could squeeze me in for dinner. I'll be in the neighborhood again. Going to finalize a big sale. You could help me celebrate. I'll give you a call."

"Okay, give me a call." Rebecca would agree to anything to get him off the phone. "If I'm free we'll have dinner."

"Hope to see you tomorrow. We've got lots to talk about before the big party." His voice, though quiet, had a menacing quality.

"Okay. Good night." This time she didn't hesitate. She replaced the receiver with a bang.

Lunch with Jake. Possible dinner with Les. She never knew people made so many plans around food. Tomorrow's meetings would put her calorie count way over her daily allowance.

Rebecca's physical therapy appointment went well. If she stayed on her present course she would be able to prepare for the fall season on time.

There were no taxis waiting outside the building so Rebecca decided to walk east on Seventy-Ninth Street. Even there she had a hard time finding a cab driver willing to take her to Brooklyn. They all used the same excuse. They were having some kind of engine trouble and were heading back to the garage, but would be happy to take her downtown. Drivers preferred in-and-out passengers for short destinations. They did better with tips that way. Out of desperation she gave up on the taxis. She walked to Lexington Avenue and took the subway. She changed trains at the Broadway-Nassau station and continued on to Brooklyn.

Today, without the hectic weekend crowd, the bakery had a friendly family feeling. Most of the tables were empty. An elderly couple occupying a corner table dunked hard rolls into their coffee. Two older ladies cleaned smudges off the display counter.

Rebecca recognized one of the counterladies from her last visit.

With her rag still in motion she looked up when Rebecca entered. "Hello. Can I help you?"

The older woman had the same sharp chiseled features as Jake. Rebecca extended her hand. "Hi, I'm Rebecca Carr. You must be Jake's grandmother."

The lady put her cloth on the counter. She wiped her hands on her apron before accepting Rebecca's hand. "Yes, yes, I know. The ballerina." She took Rebecca by the elbow and ushered her over to a table. "Come sit. I'll get you a cup of coffee. I've got the real thing brewing. Not the fancy-schmancy lattes we charge an arm and a leg for."

"No thanks. I don't want to bother you. I'm here to meet Jake."

"He's busy in the back." Jake's grandmother leaned close and whispered. "The boy's a wonderful chef but never was a good baker. But he wants to make some fancy sandwich for lunch. Focchia or something." She shrugged. "He puts tomatoes, feta cheese, and olives on the bread. In my day if you didn't put another slice of bread on top, it was called an open sandwich. Who's to say. It'll taste good. We'll eat it." She retrieved a glass coffee pot and poured two cups. "You take sugar or cream?"

"Black is fine."

"A little sugar or cream would be good for you. You girls work hard. You need the energy."

The door opened and Rebecca was saved by Lilliana's entrance.

"Becky, you're here early." Lilliana greeted her with a kiss on the forehead. "Flo, you bothering her to death?"

"No, Mrs. Fleichman has been delightful," Rebecca offered, in the other woman's defense.

"Mrs. Fleichman." The old lady bolted upright in her chair. "You call me Bubbe. Everyone does."

"I'd be honored." Rebecca reached across the table and patted Bubbe's hand.

"Such a nice young lady." Bubbe nodded at Lilliana. "Have a seat, Lil. We'll talk."

Rebecca took a sip of her coffee. Over the rim of her mug she watched the two grand dames. Like a pair of cats that swallowed mice they smiled at her. Their calm serene appearances were deceiving.

They waited for her to place the empty mug on the table before starting the questions. "So what do you think of my grandson?" Bubbe asked.

Rebecca coughed as the last swallow of coffee stuck in her throat.

"Flo, not now." Lilliana moved beside Rebecca and patted her on the back. "Becky only saw Jake once or twice."

"In my day, you had a date and you knew right away if the boy was for you or not."

"Mrs. Fleichman. I mean Bubbe. Your grandson and I didn't have a date. We had a business meeting to discuss Lilliana's problem."

"So you have no opinion of him?" Bubbe showed no sign of relenting. She changed her tactics. "Does he know what he's doing?"

Lilliana took her seat and folded her hands on the table. She too waited for Rebecca to answer.

She was forced to surrender. "He's very knowledgeable about organizing a benefit. I think his plan will work."

"He's a smart boy, my grandson."

Before the next line of interrogation could begin, Jake approached the table. He balanced a large platter in each hand. As he set them down on he table he smiled at Rebecca. "These two can be a handful when they're together."

Rebecca knew he was referring to her table companions and not to the plates in his hands.

His eyes twinkled when he addressed his grandmother and Lilliana. "Ladies, have you been bothering Miss Carr with questions she has no answers for?"

Thanks, Rebecca mouthed silently.

He inclined his head, but not before he cast a warning look at the older woman.

"We're just having a nice conversation," Bubbe defended herself. "Rebecca has just been telling us how well your plans are going. She thinks you're a real balabusta."

Lilliana nodded in agreement.

Jake's eyes shifted from one person to the other. "Is that so?" When his eyes met Rebecca's they exchanged a subtle look of amusement. He took a seat beside her. Jake leaned close and whispered. "Do you know what a balabusta is?"

"No. Should I ask her?" Rebecca said.

"Do you really want to start?"

Rebecca's laughter was her answer.

"Look, they have a secret?" Bubbe winked at Lilliana.

"Smells good," Rebecca said. Her stomach rumbled.

Bubbe must have heard the gastric grumbles. She immediately started serving the warm focaccia bread. The first two slices she cut were immense. She shoveled them onto a plate and passed it to Rebecca.

Rebecca passed the plate to Jake. He reached for it resting his hand on hers. Just his light touch made her aware of his closeness. He took the plate she handed him. "You'll scare her away if you serve portions that huge."

"I don't think she scares easy." Bubbe gave her grandson a calculating look and added, "Not like some people I know."

Jake took the serving plate from his grandmother and cut a thin slice for Rebecca.

Rebecca could feel everyone watching her. Waiting for her approval as if they had just opened an expensive bottle of wine.

She remembered how transparent she had been the first time she was alone with Jake. He had been able to easily read her thoughts. Her guard was up now. She took a bite, looked directly at Jake, and smiled. "Mmm, delicious."

He looked boyishly pleased at her response.

A bell announced a customer. Bubbe got up to serve the lady who just entered. "Here." She offered Jake her seat. "Sit across from Rebecca so you can watch her pretty face as she eats your fancy bread."

Jake stood up too but he didn't take the seat his grandmother offered. "Sit. Enjoy your lunch. I'll wait on the lady."

"Some lady," Bubbe mumbled under her breath. "She's been after my grandson ever since they were young children. Wants to make him number five."

"I thought she was married only three times," Lilliana said.

"No, no." Bubbe put another slice of bread on Rebecca's plate. "Don't you remember? She married the second husband again, after her third divorce. Three men, four marriages."

"Don't worry, Jake's not interested," Lilliana reassured her friend.

Rebecca noticed the older ladies exchange smiles and then turn their eyes in her direction. However, Rebecca was more interested in what was going on over her shoulder, at the counter, between Jake and Miss I'm Looking for Number Five.

"Jake Fleichman, what are you doing?" Miss Number Five stood with her hands folded across her chest.

"I'm filling your order."

"No, you're not. I asked for crumb buns and you're stuffing cheese danish in the bag."

"Sorry." Jake looked past the lady. Amusement flickered in the eyes that met Rebecca's glance.

"Go sit." Bubbe intervened. "You invited the ladies here to talk about your party. So go talk. I'll finish this sale."

It was obvious who was in charge here. Without hesitating, Jake removed his apron and took the seat across from Rebecca.

With expert efficiency Bubbe completed the sale and returned to the table. "Show them what you got, Lil."

Lilliana opened her pocketbook and took out an envelope. "I received this check in the mail. Imagine, someone can't come to the party so they sent me a hundred dollars."

"I'm glad to see the donations are starting to come in." Jake took a bite of the cold bread. "We'll start paying off your creditors with the early money."

"What about Les? Shouldn't we give him a little money as a show of good faith?" Rebecca asked.

Jake waited until he finished chewing before he answered. "The invitation to the party is the only thing he's going to get until all the money is in."

This made Rebecca uneasy. Les wanted to meet with her soon. He would expect her to fill him in on their progress. She was stuck between a rock and a hard place. She owed it to Jake not to revel his plans. Les knew her too well. He would know if she was holding something back.

"Don't look so worried." Lilliana reached across the table and patted Rebecca's hand. "Jake knows what he's doing."

"It's not Jake I'm concerned about." Rebecca confessed. She wanted to own up to her agreement with Les but worried that Jake wouldn't understand.

"Lilliana's right. There's nothing to worry about. I've dealt with Morgan before."

"This might be different." Rebecca wanted to ask Jake about his previous dealings with Les. But he would probably remind her it had been her idea not to get personal.

"Let him sweat a little. He doesn't have to know what we're up to." Jake stood up to clear the table.

Words stuck in Rebecca's throat. Even double agents had a go-between. Heavy steps announced another customer.

"Good afternoon, ladies and gentleman." Vinnie came right over and straddled a chair.

"Hey Vin. How did things go?" Jake said.

"Did you meet with the contractor?" Lilliana asked.

"Everything went fine." Vinnie glanced sideways at Rebecca, waiting for her question.

"She doesn't know yet," Jake said.

"What don't I know?" Rebecca raised her brows.

"Vinnie met with some construction contractors," Jake explained. "Even if the benefit raises enough money to pay off the creditors and back rent, we still have an old building to deal with."

"Shouldn't you speak with Les before you get bids from contractors?" This time Rebecca moaned. "Les will never go for us sneaking around behind his back."

"Who's gonna tell him?" Vinnie gave Rebecca a suspicious look.

"No reason to tell Les anything until we know what the plan is," Lilliana assured her accomplices.

Everyone sat silent while Jake reviewed the estimate Vinnie handed him. He jotted some words on a napkin then nodded and announced. "It's going to work. And Morgan will like it."

"What's going to work?" Rebecca asked.

Jake stood up and walked behind Rebecca. He placed his hands on her shoulders. She relaxed into the gentle massage.

"Miss Carr and I are not only going to present Mr. Morgan with a check for rent owed, we will also give him enough money to repair that rundown shack he calls a building," Jake announced to the group.

Lilliana clasped her hands together. "That will take a lot of money."

"I have a way to bring in the necessary funds." Jake sounded excited. "I'm going to auction wine from my private collection. I'll even serve it to the lucky bidder at a dinner I prepare."

"Maybe we could all donate something to be auctioned." Rebecca liked the idea. "I could get tickets to the ballet with backstage passes."

"Jake and I'll bid on that one." Vinnie winked at Rebecca. "We've never been to the ballet."

"No, we haven't." Jake rubbed his ear. "I thought we could auction some of your services as a handyman."

Vinnie nodded. "I was thinking maybe you could have the ladies bid for a date with me."

"We'll have to clean you up first." Bubbe flicked some paint off Vinnie's shirt. "What were you doing? Knocking down walls?"

"Some of the walls had weak spots." Vinnie closed his fist. "We had to see if they were worth repairing."

"You didn't." A soft gasp came from Rebecca.

"Just a little tap. Hey, I've got an idea. How about a date with the ballerina?"

Rebecca couldn't recoup quick enough to protest. Everyone seemed to have an answer.

"Such a valuable item." Bubbe pinched Rebecca's cheek.

"Better than tickets to the ballet," Lilliana said.

Rebecca could feel the heat rise in her face. She could handle standing ovations with style and grace but sitting here listening to the little group expound on her attributes was embarrassing. They spoke about her as if she wasn't there.

"How about you, boss? You'd bid for a date with the ballerina?"

"Of course he would. My grandson is not a fool."

"Well, would ya?" Vinnie persisted.

Jake stood at the head of the table with his hands joined together behind him. His chin thrust forward. Rebecca held her breath and waited for his answer.

"Of course I would. I'm committed to raising money for Lilliana."

"Such loyalty for the cause," Vinnie chided.

"No one has asked Rebecca how she feels about being auctioned," Jake said.

Rebecca found her voice quickly. "An auction is a great idea. But I'd feel like I was being sacrificed to the highest bidder."

"That settles it. The lady'd rather choose her own dates." A sarcastic but sympathetic glimmer appeared in Jake's eyes.

"I didn't say I wouldn't do it." Rebecca lifted her chin and looked directly at Jake. "You've already given us the use of your restaurant and staff. Now you're going to donate wine from your private stock."

"Your name on the invitation and your presence at the affair is your contribution." Jake looked around the table.

Everyone nodded in agreement.

"I feel like a decoration. I want to take a more active part."

"Maybe you could whip up a dessert or something," Vinnie kidded.

"I'd rather be sold to the highest bidder."

"That settles it. You, me, and Jake's expensive wine. It won't matter where the bidding starts but where it ends will be very interesting." Vinnie's mouth twitched with amusement.

Jake finished clearing the table. Rebecca offered to help. His silent coolness was evidence he was not amused. With a stack of dirty dishes he disappeared into the back of the bakery.

Rebecca hoped she hadn't acted on impulse. She was going to be mortified with a room full of men assessing her from head to toe. Even more disturbing was the thought of Jake not being the highest bidder.

"Dessert, anyone." Jake and Bubbe placed plates of assorted bakery cookies on the table.

Rebecca groaned. She would have to cancel her dinner date with Les. "Everything was delicious but I couldn't have another bite."

"Just one cookie." Bubbe passed the plate under Rebecca's nose. "How can you resist?"

"Years of training. I'm not a sweets eater."

"Maybe I should hire you for the bakery. At least I know you wouldn't be eating the profits." Bubbe tapped Vinnie's hand as he reached for a fistful of cookies. "Not like this bottomless pit. I don't know how my grandson makes so much money with this boy managing his kitchen."

Jake placed his arm around Vinnie's shoulder. "Nobody

can deal with my distributors the way my buddy does, and he doesn't eat the profits."

Vinnie tightened his belt buckle to give validity to Jake's last statement.

Rebecca got up, signaling she was ready to leave. She gathered up her pocketbook and the copy of the invitation Jake had given her.

"When all this meshugas is over, Jake can bring you to the house," Bubbe said.

Rebecca gave Bubbe a kiss. "I'd like that."

Bubbe looked sideways at her grandson. "If he doesn't bring you, come anyway."

"Are you staying?" Rebecca asked Lilliana.

"No, I'm leaving too." She linked her arm in Rebecca's and said good-bye to their hosts.

Outside the bakery they stopped for a moment. "Have you ever met anyone like him?" Lilliana asked.

"He really cares about the people in this neighborhood." Rebecca turned her face toward the window pretending to study her reflection. She watched Jake. He sat at the table with Vinnie and his grandmother. Jake poured coffee for everyone. Leisurely they sipped their drinks and nibbled on dessert. Although she could only see their lips move, it was obvious they were enjoying each others company. Jake threw back his head and laughed at something one of his companions said. In return, they smiled at his reply.

Jake looked up and met her eyes over the window sign. With two fingers to his forehead he gave her a casual salute.

Embarrassed, she turned so abruptly she almost knocked Lilliana to the ground.

"Good-looking boy." Lilliana steadied herself. "If I was younger he could cook breakfast for me any morning."

"Lil, what are you getting at?"

"I think you should try and hold on to this one."

"Hold on to what? After the benefit he goes back to his pots and pans and I go back to practices and performances." But Rebecca knew she didn't want it to end. She felt something for Jake. At first she thought it might be his zany restaurant crew or his kindhearted grandmother that made her want to be a part of Jake's world. She realized they defined Jake and made him the compassionate man she was growing attached to.

"Remember, you were the one who said, only business partners." Lilliana shook her finger at Rebecca. "Before you knew anything about him you labeled him an outsider, someone you could never be interested in."

"We'd never get together. He's busy and so am I."

Lilliana glanced down at Rebecca's leg. "You're not so busy now."

"I've never dated anyone outside the ballet."

"There's a first time for everything. Maybe he'll be the highest bidder."

"Do you think it's possible?" Rebecca's voice drifted off as she imagined herself on real date with Jake Fleichman.

"You heard the man say he's determined to help me out of this mess."

"I'm not so sure he's my type." Rebecca made another attempt to find an excuse.

"And what exactly is your type?" Lilliana raised her brow. "Was that snooty choreographer your type?"

"At least we had dance in common. Jake's never been to a ballet except for the school recital, and I don't cook."

"It is difficult stepping out into the real world. Like standing on toeshoes for the first time." Lilliana gave her a hug. "Look how successful you were at that."

Chapter Five

Rebecca's physical therapist was impressed with her improvement. He gave her permission to take a light dance class. For a few days her life was once again a routine of exercise and classes. It wasn't enough. She tried to blame the emptiness on the absence of her ballet friends. Just over the bridge, Brooklyn and Jake seemed so far away.

After several days of telephone tag she spoke to Les. She was relieved to hear he was too busy to meet her. He had some last minute summer rentals to show out on Long Island and wouldn't be back in the city until just before the benefit.

Two days before the benefit Jake called. "Haven't heard from you in a few days. I thought the little group at the bakery may have scared you away."

"I don't scare easily. I assumed the plans were going smoothly."

"They are." Jake cleared his throat. "Thought you might like to join Jewel and me for an early breakfast."

"How early?" Rebecca had a dilemma. She wanted to accept his invitation without sounding too enthusiastic.

"Can you be at the restaurant around six?"

"In the morning?"

"Have to get to the green market early if we want to pick the best produce. We'll eat while we shop."

This was definitely going to be a new experience for Rebecca. "What are you shopping for?"

"Ingredients for Friday night. Before you eat you have to shop." He made the whole cooking process sound so simple.

"See you in the morning." Rebecca had promised Lilliana she wouldn't refuse any invitations from Jake. Could her conniving old friend be behind this impromptu date? If she was, did Jake realize it and decide to bring his daughter along as a chaperone?

The market was beginning to come alive. Flower vendors arranged kaleidoscopes of fresh-picked blossoms. Trucks packed to the rooftop with crates and burlap bags of summer fruits and vegetables were being unloaded and set up for display.

Jewel took Rebecca by the hand and steered her through the crowd that had already filled the rows between the stalls. Jake had his shopping route perfected and disappeared.

"Dad is like a madman on the loose when he comes here. Stay with me."

Rebecca was glad for the child's company. Jewel was definitely more comfortable than Rebecca as they weaved between shoppers laden with early-morning purchases.

"Hey, Jewel." A vendor motioned them toward his stand. "Your dad abandon you already? Tell him when he's done with Eric I've got something he'll like." The man held up what looked like a squash. "New this season. It's a peppermint squash." His fingernails were short and trim but still stained with the black dirt of his labor. He traced the thick green and yellow stripes.

"Are those Sarah's scones?" Jewel asked.

"Baked fresh last night. Try some with peach butter."

Rebecca was amazed at how quickly Jewel had her scone buttered and ready to eat.

"What about you, lady? Don't you want to try one of my wife's scones?"

"Had breakfast already," Rebecca lied. All she had was her usual eye-opening cup of black coffee.

Jewel came to her rescue. "Miss Becky's a ballerina. Has to stay in shape for the season."

"How about some fruit?" The vendor handed Rebecca a peach.

She bit into the succulent peach. She wasn't prepared for the sweet tenderness teasing her taste buds. Some of the juice dripped down her chin.

"How's it taste?" Jake stood behind her. He handed her a napkin. "Worth buying?"

Rebecca nodded. She had never tasted such fresh fruit flavor. She was afraid to open her mouth. Before she could speak, Jewel distracted Jake.

"Dad, look at the great squash Jim has and you've got to taste Sarah's peach butter."

Rebecca watched Jake examine the striped vegetable. He held one up to the morning light. With care he replaced it. "I'll take five pounds. They'll be a big hit at the benefit dinner."

"What kind of benefit you doing this time?" the vendor asked.

"My associate and I are raising money for a local ballet school."

"Nice associate." He winked at Rebecca. "What else you need today?"

"The usual. Some of those giant portobellos and those first-class tomatoes you haven't unpacked."

Mushrooms the size of small frisbees were displayed next to an assortment of red, yellow, and—something Rebecca had never seen before—purple tomatoes. Jake waited for Jim to produce a crate of oversized beefsteaks. A young couple with a baby stroller watched Jake sort through the basket.

"Are these good for sauce?" the woman asked.

"My heirloom tomatoes, a sauce? Never. No sale." Jim pulled the crate away.

"Don't pay attention to him. He's a little protective when it comes to some of his vegetables," Jake said. "Don't overdress these tomatoes. All these need is a drizzle of olive oil and some salt and pepper to bring out the flavor."

Rebecca listened too as Jake explained which tomatoes would make a good sauce and which would be better in a salad. A little crowd gathered arond the produce stand as he described how he would sauté the zucchini with yellow squash and shallots.

His hands already full with vegetables, Jake snatched another tomato. He juggled the vegetables as he spoke. The crowd was delighted. He tossed a zucchini to Jewel.

She too held a vegetable in each hand. "Ready, Dad?"

Jake concentrated for a moment on the objects suspended in air. He nodded. Jewel tossed him another tomato. Before it landed, he tossed the zuchinni in his left hand to his right hand. After a few moments juggling on his own, he threw his daughter a squash. In rapid succession Jewel tossed them back. They never missed a beat. Like street performers, they played the crowd.

Jake was enjoying himself. Rebecca understood the elated expression on Jake's face as his appreciative audience cheered him on. Even she believed he was about to conjure up his pots and pans and prepare a meal for everyone.

Unprepared for his next move, Rebecca had no time to object when Jake nodded for her take Jewel's place. She had been watching Jewel closely.

Jake continued to juggle. "Just catch what I throw and toss it back to my left hand."

Jake juggled for three beats and Rebecca prepared for her next catch. They continued for several more minutes. It was so easy. Rebecca couldn't remember when she had had so much fun. For a brief moment she lost her concentration. She missed a beat. Tomatoes, zucchini and squash tumbled to the ground. Jake retrieved them, placed them off to the side and joined hands with his fellow performers. They bowed to their audience.

"Your little performance gathered a nice crowd." Jim handed Jake a scone. "Breakfast is on me."

Jake offered the scone to Jewel.

"They ate already." Jim informed him. "Your daughter had a scone and the ballerina had a peach." Jim motioned for Jake to step closer and whispered in his ear. "A scone wouldn't hurt. She could use a little meat on her bones."

Even though Jim spoke in a whisper Rebecca heard his last comment. It didn't bother her. She was getting used to Jake's friends and family trying to put meat on her bones. Only Jake didn't force the issue. She wanted to believe it was because he liked her lean dancer's body. It was more likely he was just honoring the terms of her agreement and avoiding any personal comments. Maybe it was time for Jake Fleichman to be a little bit less honorable.

Jake walked around the produce stand to gather his purchases. A well-dressed elderly woman approached Rebecca and Jewel. "Your little show was delightful." She pinched Jewel's cheek. "You have a very attractive family."

"Oh no, we're . . ." Rebecca began to explain but the lady had joined the other customers who were anxious to pay for their purchases.

Jewel was at the butter display. Rebecca joined her. They each bought a jar of peach butter. Jewel's was for her great-grandmother. Rebecca bought one for Lilliana. It would be proof she had actually spent the morning with Jake.

With bundles securely tucked in their arms, they followed Jake to the car. Rebecca was surprised at how carefree and easy the whole shopping experience had been.

"Great juggling, Miss Becky," Jewel said. Then she turned to Jake. "Hey Dad. Don't you think we should invite her to more market days?"

For a moment Jake said nothing. "That's up to Miss Becky. I don't know if she wants to spend more time with us."

If Jake wanted to see her after the benefit was over he sure had an unusual way of asking. The morning had been fun. Even the crowds didn't bother her. "I'd love to do this again."

"I shop every morning. Just give me a call."

As they approached Jake's van, Rebecca shielded her eyes from the morning sun. "Is that Les leaning against the van?"

"I've seen strange things at the market but this takes the cake." Jake was as surprised as she was to see Les.

"What are you doing here?" Rebecca asked.

"I came back from Long Island last night and wanted to make sure I got in touch with Fleichman."

"How did you know we'd be here?"

"I'm pleasantly surprised to find you here too. I knew Fleichman would be here. All the great chefs shop the greenmarkets," Les said with heavy sarcasm.

"Thanks for the compliment, Morgan, but what's on your mind?" Jake walked around to the back of the van. He placed his morning purchases inside.

Morgan followed him. "I'll get right to the point. When I was out in the Hamptons I met a man. An editor of a local magazine. I told him about your little benefit."

"That was very nice of you. Did he make a check out to you?" Jake didn't try to keep the sarcasm from his voice.

"You have no faith in me, Fleichman."

"Les, what is all this about?" Rebecca was curious.

Jake rested against the van with his arms folded across his chest. Les's presence seemed to amuse him. "Get to the point."

"The man wants to do a piece on us."

"Us?" Rebecca asked.

"Yes. Three kids from the old neighborhood get together to help save a local dance school," Les said.

Jake slipped his arm around her waist and positioned her next to him against the van. "Let's hear what the man has to say. I'm sure it gets better."

Rebecca noticed Les's look at Jake's hand placed possessively around her waist. She felt her checks turn the color of radishes.

"Okay, what have you planned?" she asked, avoiding Les's smirk.

"I've given your little party some thought and decided I'd like to do my share." He looked directly at Rebecca. "I know what the school means to you."

"If you want to help, why don't you just forgive Lilliana's overdue rent and fix up the building," Jake said.

"Now Fleichman, you know I can't do that. My other tenants would expect me to make similar concessions. You can't run your restaurant giving away free food."

Rebecca stepped off to the side. She stood next to Jewel and listened as the men engaged in a somewhat friendly banter.

"Dad and Mr. Morgan never agree on anything."

"Why do they act like this?" Rebecca felt ridiculous asking the child such a question.

Jewel shrugged. "I don't know." Obviously not interested in the converstation, she climbed into the van.

Rebecca rejoined the men just in time to hear the details of Les's plan.

"I've arranged a photo shoot on the Brooklyn Bridge, to go along with the story. If we could all show up tomorrow in professional attire, it would add a nice touch."

"Tomorrow. You have permits and everything?" Rebecca asked.

"Fleichman is not the only one with friends in the Mayor's office."

"But it's the day of the benefit. I'm sure Jake has a million things to do." She turned to face Jake. "Don't you?"

"If Morgan went to all this trouble, I can spare a few hours. My crew can handle things." Jake spoke directly to Morgan. "I'll be there in my tunic and my tallest chef hat."

"You will?" The surprise was evident in Les's voice. "I mean, that's great. You'll be there too, won't you, Becky?"

Rebecca was standing close enough to Jake to feel his muscles tense when Les called her by the name reserved for her students and old friends.

"Will there be a changing area? I can't prance around Brooklyn in a tutu."

"Absolutely. I'll see you at nine. We'll be shooting from the center of the bridge."

When Les was out of sight, Rebecca said, "That Les, he's always full of surprises."

"A little odd for Morgan to have a sudden change of heart." Jake rearranged the bundles in the back of his van. "Maybe he's gotten wind of our plans to restore the building and he sees things in a more profitable light."

"Who could have shared that information with him?" Rebecca asked. She was glad she had not been able to meet with Les. She would have felt terribly guilty if she had been responsible for leaking information.

"We'll find out more tomorrow." Jake turned on the car ignition.

"Can I come too?" Jewel asked from the back seat.

"It's going to be a quick shoot and I've got to go back to the restaurant."

"Then we'll have to do a Brooklyn Bridge day and invite Miss Becky," Jewel said.

Although Rebecca didn't look at Jake, she sensed his eyes on her. She turned to listen to his daughter. "That's very sweet. But what's a Brooklyn Bridge day?"

"Dad and I take the subway to the Manhattan side and walk back to Brooklyn."

"Would you believe I never walked over the bridge," Rebecca said.

"Never?" Jewel's eyes were the size of giant portobellos. "Oohh. Let's do it today."

"Not today, we have too much to do." Jake pulled out of the parking spot.

"You're right, Dad. We wouldn't want her to miss breakfast at Mort's."

"What's Mort's?" Rebecca asked.

"Are you sure you're from Brooklyn?" Jewel asked.

"I grew up in Brooklyn. Not far from your dad but I didn't spend much time there."

"You knew my dad when he was a kid?" Jewel could hardly contain her excitement.

"No, we didn't." Rebecca wished she had known Jake. "Tell me about Mort's."

"They make the best chocolate-chip pancakes in the world."

"Oh. Sounds good." Rebecca tried to echo the child's excitement.

"Don't tell me you never had chocolate-chip pancakes." Jewel giggled. "Where did you find her, Dad?"

"The usual place. Bubbe's bakery."

Rebecca enjoyed the playful banter between father and daughter. "I'd love to join you." If she watched her calorie intake for a day she might even indulge in Mort's infamous pancakes.

"Great, it's a date." Jake said.

Rebecca smiled to herself. Lilliana would be thrilled to hear Rebecca was about to take several giant steps into the real world.

Chapter Six

"I can't believe it," Jake moaned, as he slowed the van down to a crawl on Eighty-Sixth Street.

"What's wrong, Dad?" Jewel asked.

"There's a FOR RENT sign in the window of Angelo's Butcher. I can't believe it."

As they crawled past, Rebecca stretched her neck out the window. "Isn't there some other butcher shop you can go to? Don't they all make sausage?"

"You don't understand. Angelo's family has been in Bensonhurst for generations. It's a crime. Nobody makes pancetta like old man Angelo," Jake said, as if the answer were obvious.

"I'm sure the benefit will be a success even without Mr. Angelo's pan. . . ." Rebecca tried to sound reassuring.

"Pancetta." Jake corrected. "With *A Taste of Brooklyn* as

our theme, we have to have Brooklyn's best sample of ethnic foods."

"I know you're busy, but maybe you can make it yourself."

The traffic light turned red. "Have you ever tasted really good sausage?" One hand on the steering wheel, with the other he clasped Rebecca's knee. "Let me answer that. You don't eat sausage."

Rebecca nodded in agreement.

"How can I explain this to you. It has to do with texture, consistency, and taste." His staff would be rolling and cutting pasta dough for days. The least he could do was provide the best ingredients available to fill the delicate ravolis they would create. "You can't prepare a great dish with second-rate ingredients. Hors d'oeuvres set the tone for the entire meal. They are labor intensive. Think of them as little pieces of art."

Again Jake noticed the lost look on her face. "You don't eat appetizers either." This time it was more a statement than a question.

"I try to avoid them. They're small but deadly. Those calories can add up fast."

He knew Rebecca was trying to understand what he was saying. "There must be a ballet dancer who has a signature number only she can perform." Jake changed his analogy. "Hard as you try, it can't be recreated with the same degree of accuracy."

"They say no one can dance *The Dying Swan* like Anna Pavlova," Rebecca said.

"Exactly. Once you've seen her you don't want to ruin that perfection."

There was a soft whimper from the back of the car.

"Did I say something wrong?" Jake asked.

"She's been dead a long time, Dad."

"You do get my point."

"Point gotten." Rebecca patted the hand still resting on her knee.

"Santacrose makes a decent luiganigo, a fresh pork sausage." Jake made a left turn and headed for Bay Ridge.

The back of the van already overflowed with breads from Flatbush, jerk chicken from East New York, and pelmeni from Brighton Beach. No wonder the response had been so favorable. Jake knew his business. The rich and even the not-so-rich jumped at the chance to attend one of his closed parties.

Santacrose's Sausage Shop had the similar look of the delis and specialty shops they had already visited. However, finding a parking spot was a little difficult. Jake slowed the van to a crawl and tried to glance in the window.

"Want me to get out and see who's inside?" Jewel asked. She ran out of the van and strolled by the storefront. She casually peeked in the window before running back to report to Jake. "She's there."

Jake slammed his open palms against the steering wheel. "Just what I was afraid of."

"Is there another problem?" Rebecca asked. "Who don't you want to see?"

"Maria makes Dad nervous."

Rebecca looked at Jake. A worried brow made his face tense. "I didn't think it was possible for anyone to do that to your father."

"Maria can. She's always trying to fix him up. Meet my niece Toni. A beautiful girl." Jewel wrinkled her face. "Right, Toni looked like she had three eyes." Jewel chat-

tered on and on about the shopkeepers and their monster-
like nieces.

"Is there someone else we can get good sausage from?"
Rebecca asked.

"We're here, I'll deal with it." Jake sent Jewel into the
shop with instructions to tell Joe her father was looking for
a parking spot. As she walked away he shouted, "Tell him
I've got a special friend with me." He said the next words
tentatively as if testing an idea. "Maybe you can help."

"What do you have in mind?" Rebecca asked.

"Remember the old lady at the market."

"She thought we were married." Rebecca hadn't thought
he heard the lady's comment. "You want me to pretend I'm
your wife."

"No, no, just a friend. A girlfriend." Jake was having a
hard time saying the words. "I'd owe you big for this."

Rebecca couldn't believe the demons that haunted Jake
had this kind of effect on him. The man was petrified by
the thought of a relationship.

There was something she wanted from Jake. She had just
been handed the opportunity to negotiate.

"I understand how you feel." She was careful not to re-
veal her delight at being handed this silver platter. "I think
we can help each other. We're both in a similar situation.
Being on an auction block makes me uncomfortable. If the
final bid could come from someone I already knew, I'd feel
better."

"Are you asking me to be the high bidder at the benefit
auction?" A corner of his mouth twitched with the beginning of a smile.

"Is that such an unpleasant thought?" She asked.

"Not at all." He looked at her critically but smiled ap-
provingly. "But why me? Why not your friend Morgan?"

"Les and I are old friends. We have dates all the time. He wouldn't bid on something he could get for free." She looked directly at Jake. "However, he might join the bidding if he was competing against you."

Just as she was beginning to feel a bit sorry for putting him on the spot, Jake accepted her offer.

"I could never let him win." He offered her a sudden dazzling smile and his hand. "It's a deal."

"Let's see what your performance in there is worth." Jake came around the van and helped Rebecca out.

Arm in arm with broad smiles on their faces they walked toward the deli. To passerby they appeared like lovers who had just shared an intimate joke.

"Ciao, ciao." A robust man in a white butcher apron rushed forward to greet them. "The bambina was starving so Maria made her one of our special sandwiches. You'll join her." Joe motioned toward a corner table where Maria was fussing over Jewel. The child was busy devouring an overstuffed sandwich cut from a crusty loaf of Italian bread.

Jake pulled out a chair for Rebecca. He almost fell off the seat next to her when she took his hand and gave it a tender squeeze.

The introductions were made. Mr. Santacrose pinched Rebecca's cheek. "Que bella. Just as pretty as my wife's niece."

Jewel looked at Rebecca and rolled her eyes. In return, Rebecca rubbed the spot between her eyes. They both laughed.

Joe passed around crusty slices of bread and slivers of spicy sausage. "Try this fenocchiona. Put it on a slice of bread."

"This bread is a perfect balance to the spice in the salami." Jake put his fingers to his lips. "Bellisimo."

"How much you need?" Joe asked.

"Actually I'm here for some mortadella and luganiga." Jake followed Joe to the counter. Rebecca followed and slipped her arm through Jake's. He acknowledged her part in his little charade with a smile. His plan worked like a charm. He watched her face as she listened to Joe explain the fine art of making sausage.

"The boys in Jake's kitchen make a beautiful bumble bee ravioli. Filled with my sausage, it's like heaven." Joe sighed. "Even my Maria hasn't been able to master the technique. We all have our secrets." Joe walked behind the counter. "Sausage you need. My mortadella you need." He nodded in Rebecca's direction. "My single nieces you don't need."

Jake laughed along with Joe. "Someday we'll tell each other about our secret ingredients and techniques."

Some neighborhood women formed a line behind them. Maria waited on them. She offered samples of cheese and cold cuts to everyone.

Jake reached across the counter for a slice of sharp provolone. "Taste this." He offered Rebecca a sample of the cheese.

She took a nibble. "Hmm, it's strong." A crumb rested on the corner of her mouth. With the tip of her tongue she traced the outline of her lips, only a smudge of cheese remained.

Jake's finger made a path to the tantalizing spot. His pulse quickened. He removed his finger from her lip and placed his arm around her waist. She edged a little closer. She was enjoying their little charade and so was he. It all felt so natural.

Laden with their purchases they walked toward the van, when Maria came running after them. "Take this, take this."

She handed Jewel a bag. "Fresh-baked biscotti. Some cookies to snack on for the ride home." Before disappearing into the crowded store she turned and shouted over her shoulder. "You got a nice girl there, Jake. Good luck."

"You guys were great." Jewel had obviously enjoyed their little deception. "You had everyone believing you were dating or something."

Rebecca took a graceful bow. "A command performance at your father's request." The sincerity of her smile made Jake's defenses melt.

He tucked the last package into the ice chest. Beside him Rebecca looked radiant. The success of their charade had made them both feel good. Jake could not recall a more memorable market day. His next action surprised him more than anyone. He placed his open palm around Rebecca's neck and drew her close. Just before he placed his lips on hers he noticed Jewel's face pressed against the back window. His lips found Rebecca's cheek instead. "Thanks, I owe you one."

Chapter Seven

"Can Miss Becky have dinner with us tonight?" Jewel had unwrapped Maria's biscotti and had already devoured half the bag.

Rebecca wondered where the child put all the food she had consumed this morning. "How can you be thinking of dinner? Didn't you have enough to eat?"

"Miss Becky's right. Put those cookies away before you get sick." Jake glanced at his watch. "It's getting late. I've spent more time than usual away from the restaurant. They're probably waiting for me to approve tonight's menus before they're sent off to the printer."

"I've got things to do too." Rebecca regarded him sympathetically. Her little act had thrown him into internal chaos. She felt his body tense every time she touched him or moved in too close. He most likely needed an emotional resting place, somewhere he could safely sort out his feelings. In his restaurant, surrounded by his crew, he would be secure. Would Jake be thinking about her?

"Can I drop you off at the subway station?" Jake asked.

"I would prefer to call a cab."

"She can do that from our house." Jewel's bottom lip turned out in a pleading pout. "She can meet Mrs. Lopez and Tina."

"Our housekeeper and the cat." Jake had the look of surrender on his face.

Rebecca got the impression he felt like his only ally had just turned to the other side. "I'd love to meet Tina and your housekeeper."

They turned off Montague Street onto a magical tree-shaded block from another era. As they drove past a row of brownstones and townhouses Rebecca had a feeling of déjà vu. Some of the stage crew lived in the Heights but she had never been invited to their apartments. She spent so little time in Brooklyn she had no explanation for the strong feeling this street provoked.

Jake pulled to a stop in front of a magnificent four-story townhouse. "I'll drop you ladies off. Sorry I can't stay and offer you the grand tour."

"No problem. I'm just going to meet Jewel's cat, call for a cab, and be on my way too."

"No, no, you've got to come in and see the view." Jewel took her hand and pulled her toward the stoop.

The feeling of déjà vu was stronger than before. Rebecca knew exactly what the view would be. A huge window would overlook the promenade onto the river. Above the river the Manhattan skyline would rise from the shore. If she looked to the left the Statue of Liberty presided over the harbor. To the right she'd see the massive cables of the

Brooklyn Bridge. She suddenly knew why this prime real estate was so familiar. She felt the color drain from her face. All her attention focused on the building. She was unaware of a crack in the cement.

"You okay?" Jake held her elbow to steady her. "I've got to get this repaved."

"You own this building?"

"The whole thing. We live on the top two floors and rent out the lower apartments."

Years ago Les had shown her this building. The previous owner had gutted the inside but ran out of money before completing the project. Les entered a closed bid. His bid was too low. The sale went to a higher bidder. Les was devasted. She never understood his disappointment until now.

Jake Fleichman had won the bid. She was beginning to understand the rivalry between the two men. She hoped she wasn't setting them up for one more competition the night of the banquet.

Jewel raced up the stairs ahead of them. Before anyone could join her she reached for the note tacked to the door. "Gee Dad, Mrs. Lopez is out. This note says she'll pick me up at the restaurant."

"I'll have to take you with me." Jake walked back to the van."

"Oh no. I can't. You were right, I had one cookie too many." Jewel doubled over clutching her stomach. "I think I'll be sick if I get back in the car. I can't go to the restaurant. The smell of food. . . ." She burped.

"You can't stay home alone." Surprised and concerned, Jake looked at his daughter.

"Maybe Miss Becky could stay with me until you get

back." With big sad eyes she looked up at her dance teacher.

Rebecca didn't know much about kids but she had never seen anyone get sick so fast. Just a moment ago Jewel raced up the stairs. She had barely digested her last meal and she was discussing dinner plans.

Jake combed his fingers through his hair. "Would it be a big imposition?"

"Not at all," Rebecca said. "I just have a light workout to do."

"Do you workout every evening?" he asked.

"I have to when I'm not performing."

"There's a gym off my bedroom. Help Miss Becky find whatever she needs."

"Sure, Dad." Jewel suddenly got the sparkle back in her eyes. "Why don't you give Mrs. Lopez the night off?"

"We'll see." Jake gave his daughter a curious look.

Rebecca was a little disappointed when Jake didn't bother coming in with them. He had double-parked and didn't want to risk getting a ticket.

Jewel had made a sudden recovery and was more than capable of giving Rebecca the grand tour. Light from the picture windows overlooking the East River gave depth to the narrow rooms. An open kitchen dominated the living space on the lower level. There was no doubt this room belonged to Jake. Hard durable stainless steel counters and appliances outlined the area. They were functional—just what was needed to get the job done.

"Want to eat? I'm hungry," Jewel announced.

"How can you be hungry?" Rebecca asked. "I thought you didn't feel well. Anyway, we can call out."

"You don't cook?"

Seeing Jewel's amusement made Rebecca laugh. She

took the child's hand and followed her into the kitchen. "Okay, show me what Mrs. Lopez would make for dinner."

Jewel pulled a stool over to the refrigerator. "It's easy." She swung open the freezer door, revealing rows of neatly stacked packages of frozen food. "You take one from this pile and read the directions. Then take a sauce from this pile and cook it."

How simple the child made it sound.

Everything was wrapped in white paper and plastic wrap. Unlike Rebecca's freezer, this one was filled to capacity. It was the neatest freezer Rebecca had ever seen. Afraid to upset the order she took the package closest to her. A label described the contents. Baked chicken. Another label gave directions. Heat with orange glaze.

She put it back, slammed the door, turned to Jewel, and asked, "Can you nuke them?"

Jewel puckered her lips. Rebecca should have known the child of a world-famous chef had every meal cooked to perfection.

The huge stove took up most of the opposite wall. Four large burners and a monstrous grill glared at her. Using that ogre was definitely beyond Rebecca's cooking repertoire.

She began opening cabinets, not quite sure what she was looking for. Something easy, already prepared, and no mess.

To her surprise, Jewel placed an array of cereals on the table. She had already poured a mix of marshmallow stars and red, white, and blue pebbles into an oversized bowl.

Rebecca's stomach rumbled, reminding her she too had not eaten since their jumbled sampling of Italian bread, cheese, and pelmeni.

"Oh well," she said. "Might as well join the natives." She filled her bowl with the colorful grains.

Together they carried their simple feast into the living room. They put their feet up on the coffee table and turned on the TV. Rebecca couldn't remember the last time she spent such a casual evening. After rehearsals or a performance she usually picked up a salad on her way home, watched some television, and fell asleep. The next day she repeated the same routine. Although she missed the members of her company, this unplanned vacation was turning out to be very interesting.

Jewel cuddled against Rebecca and feel asleep. With her arm wrapped securely around her young pupil, Rebecca had never felt so content. She watched a black and white sitcom on TV. When it was over she noticed the lights of lower Manhattan were on across the river.

With a gentle nudge she woke Jewel. "Time to go to bed."

"Can't I wait for Dad?"

"Do you usually?"

"No. Are you going to use the exercise room?"

"I'd like to," Rebecca said.

"Great." Jewel ran over to the desk. "I'll sleep in Dad's bed tonight." She took a stick-on note pad from the top drawer.

"Are you going to leave your dad a note?"

"Sort of." Jewel handed Rebecca some paper. "Do you have any lipstick?"

Rebecca searched through her satchel and found a tube of bright red lipstick. "What do you need this for?"

"We're going to put a print of our lips on each page." Jewel started to apply her lipstick. "Then we'll leave a paper trail to Dad's room so he'll know where to find us when he comes home."

"Couldn't you just leave a note?"

"No, this is more fun. Besides, if I'm sleeping he won't have to wake me for a good night kiss." She handed the tube of lipstick to Rebecca. "Now it's your turn put your lips on the paper."

Rebecca freshened her lips. She took one note page and lightly pressed her lips to the paper. "How's this?"

"Fine, do some more." There was a mischievous twinkle in the child's eyes. "It's not like you're really kissing my dad."

"Do you do this often?" She hoped Jewel didn't notice her blush. She would be lying if she said she didn't want to be kissed by Jewel's dad. She wondered if he knew it.

"Only for special occasions."

"What's so special about today?" Rebecca asked.

"Nothing." Jewel gathered up their paper kisses. Her lips had left sweet little flutters on the bright yellow pages in contrast to the soft fullness of Rebecca's mouth. "Follow me." Jewel led the way up to the next level.

"Where do you sleep?" Rebecca asked.

"Over there." Jewel pointed to the room down the hall.

The walls of the long narrow hallway were lined with photographs. Rebecca studied the pictures. They were mostly shots of Jewel. There were some of her with Jake or Bubbe and even Vinnie. The one that Rebecca studied the longest was a baby photo of Jewel and an attractive young woman.

"That's my mom."

Rebeca knew she had no right to pry but her curiosity got the better of her. "Do you see her often?"

"In the summer. She has a very busy schedule." Jewel raced on ahead. "The gym's through there."

Rebecca didn't realize she would have to go through the

master suite to get to the exercise room. She hesitated. Entering Jake's bedroom felt like an invasion of his privacy.

Jewel rushed past. In a hurry to place the paper kisses she grabbed Rebecca by the arm and pulled her over the threshold. "The gym's over there. You going to exercise in your jeans?"

Rebecca went downstairs to get her bag. When she returned Jewel had climbed into the massive heavy wooden bed that dominated the room. With the covers tucked neatly around her, her sleepy eyes fought to stay awake. So innocent and peaceful. Rebecca couldn't help but wonder why the child lived with her father and not her mother.

Rebecca slipped on an oversized T-shirt and pulled up a pair of leg warmers. The lady's photo, the paper kisses, and the uncomfortable feeling of being in Jake's bedroom were soon forgotten in the intensity of her workout.

Jake smiled as he retrieved each paper kiss. Jewel hadn't played this game in a long time. He stopped at the end of the trail. It looked so natural, his daughter asleep in his bed and Rebecca exercising in the gym. She appeared so engrossed in her routine that he didn't want to break the spell. One hand rested on the back of a chair. Her free arm glided in a fluid motion into the air. He leaned against the door, amazed at how gracefully she completed the strenuous routine.

As she bent and glided, her much too large T-shirt did little to conceal her body. He shifted his weight for a better view. The wood boards squeaked under his feet.

"I didn't hear you come up." Rebecca stood straight up as if an imaginary string ran from the top of her to her toes.

"I didn't mean to sneak up on you. I was enjoying your routine. Don't stop on my account."

"It's nothing." She inhaled deeply to catch her breath. "Just some simple barre exercises." Rebecca took a towel from her bag and wiped the glistening moisture from her face.

"They didn't look so simple to me." Using the doorframe as his barre, Jake tried to imitate the way she stood with her feet turned in first position. "Ow, that really stretches the muscles. I can understand how you injured your leg."

His futile attempt at a plié amused her. He knew he was in trouble when her brilliant black eyes sparkled as she laughed.

"I'm done." She extended her hands to him. "Want to give it a try?"

Jake motioned to his baggy chef's pants and tunic. "I'm not dressed for this."

"What do you have on under that shirt?"

"Skin."

"That'll do." She gestured at his pants. "Take off the shirt."

"How can a man refuse a request like that." He flexed his muscles and tightened his already rippled abs.

Her smile told him she approved. "Aren't chefs suppose to be fat? What's the expression?"

"Never trust a skinny chef," Jake said. He pinched her waist. "Who's the skinny one?"

"I'm not the chef." She giggled.

"I could teach you a thing or two in the kitchen."

"This time I'm the teacher and you're the pupil."

Jake tossed his tunic across the floor. "I'm all yours."

Her smile was warm and inviting. With one finger she motioned for him to step closer. He stood behind her. She positioned his hands on her waist then encouraged him to follow her steps. It amazed him how her feet seemed to be drifting along on a cloud.

"I can't do this." Two simple steps and Jake felt like he was going to tumble forward.

She released his hands. "You did good." Crosslegged she lowered herself to the floor. She pulled her shirt over her knees.

Using the wall to support his back he sat down next to her. "Thanks for staying with Jewel."

"It was fun. Actually the whole day was surprisingly pleasant." Her smile was sincere, almost apologetic. "You really know a lot about food and parties."

"It's what I do best." He was glad she no longer had any doubts about his motives.

"I wish I could be more of a help tomorrow," Rebecca said.

Was it Jake's imagination or was the room getting smaller. They seemed to be inching closer to each other with every word.

"Is everything ready?" Rebecca asked.

"Just a few kinks to work out."

"There's one big kink we didn't plan on," Rebecca said.

"You mean the photo shoot?" He smiled, hoping to convince himself Morgan's unexpected interest in the event didn't bother him.

"You've got so much to do tomorrow. I think Les did this on purpose." Without changing her position Rebecca reached into her satchel. Jake expected her to pull out some instrument of torture. Instead she produced a bag of oranges slices.

"What are you going to do with those?" He watched her peel the fruit from its skin with delicate little bites. He needed a distraction. Keep talking about Morgan, he told himself.

"I always eat oranges after a workout." She held the empty peel up to his lips. "Want a taste?"

"I'd love to." He could bearly contain himself as he slipped his arm around her shoulder. His lips tingled with the need to taste the sweet nectar. Rebecca put down the orange peel. She didn't move. She was so close he could smell the citrus. His hand caressed behind her neck as he drew her close. He tasted the sweetness still lingering on her lips.

"Tastes delicious." His lips brushed against hers as he spoke.

"Want another taste?" she whispered.

His mouth covered hers hungrily. He was both shocked and pleased at her eagerness. His mouth dictated and hers responded.

In the other room Jake's bed creaked, reminding them they were not alone. In her sleep Jewel sighed. There was an innocent smile on her face.

"She must be having a sweet dream," Rebecca whispered.

"A very sweet dream, I'm sure." Jake pulled Rebecca closer. He could not resist tasting her lips one more time. The orange no longer lingered. The nectar had been absorbed by his kisses, leaving her lips warm and moist.

"I think you should put the sleeping princess in her own bed." Rebecca kissed his chin.

"You're right. I'll be right back." He scooped his daughter in his arms and left the room.

Almost at the door to her room Jewel rubbed the sleep from her eyes and said, "Hi, Dad. Did you find the kisses Miss Becky and I left for you?"

"Yes, I did." He tucked the covers tight and secure. "Go back to sleep. We've got a busy day tomorrow." It was amazing how quickly a child could fall back to sleep. Jake placed a kiss on the sleeping child's forehead and tiptoed out of the room.

Just before entering his bedroom he spotted a lone paper kiss on the floor. The bright red outline was full and inviting. He leaned against the wall. A part of him wanted to believe that after only a couple of weeks his feelings for Rebecca Carr were clear and real. The other part left him with a heavy doubt.

After tomorrow night there would be no reason to see her again. Then he remembered the auction. He had promised to be the high bidder and wouldn't go back on his word. He wondered if she would enjoy a private dinner at the Bridge Cafe. It would have to be soon, before her dance friends returned and she became absorbed in her professional life. He had lost his heart once to a woman whose career meant more to her than her family. He couldn't let that happen again. His fingers tightened, crushing the notepaper in his fist.

Rebecca peaked her head out the door. "Is everything okay?"

"She's sleeping." He couldn't help noticing she had changed back into her jeans and blouse. He hated to admit the impact their kisses had. They had definitely crossed over the line, separating business and pleasure.

"I called a cab." She lifted her satchel onto her shoulder. "It should be here momentarily."

"I'll wait outside with you." He took the large bag from her and lead the way down the four flights of stairs.

At the front door she reached for the doorknob. Her hand rested there for a moment. She turned to face him. For a brief second he thought he glimpsed hesitation or doubt in her usually serene features. She searched his face for an answer he didn't have. Perhaps she realized he didn't have an explanation or one she wanted to hear. Her expression became bittersweet. She turned the knob and stepped outside. The taxi was already waiting at the curb.

Rebecca stepped in and announced her destination. "Sixty-Third Street and Broadway." The meter started ticking.

There was no time to explain what had happened in the gym. Jake wanted the chance to set things straight. To tell her they might be making a mistake. Perhaps they had confused their passion for the event with what they believed they were feeling for each other. He doubted she would believe him. He wasn't sure he believed it. Whichever was true, he was not going to spend a very restful night.

Chapter Eight

The busy kitchen echoed with the sounds of its occupants as they prepared gourmet delights for the evening's gala. When Jake Fleichman threw a party, he expected perfection. Pots bubbled and pans sizzled with treats to impress even the pickiest epicurean.

"Hey boss, take it easy. You're overwhipping the cream." Vinnie looked over Jake's shoulder into the mixer bowl. "It's turning yellow."

"Darn it." Determined to correct his mistake, he beat the sides of the bowl with a vengeance. "I can still save it. I'll whip it into butter." Jake made a futile attempt at saving the cream, but he could hardly think straight. Being with Rebecca yesterday made him realize he had avoided women for too long. But other women didn't make him feel like this. He couldn't remember being so enchanted by anyone.

Vinnie took the bowl from Jake and handed it to a salad boy. "See what you can do with this."

Jake stopped short at the kitchen door. The salad boy stared blankly into the overbeaten bowl of cream.

Jake tousled the boy's hair. "Add some sun-dried tomatoes and fresh basil just before it's served. No one will ever suspect it wasn't meant to be an herb butter. Place it next to the bread from Santacrose's. If anyone asks who made the delicious spread, tell them you did."

Jake directed his next question to Vinnie. "The bread's here, isn't it?"

"Yes, yes, everything is running as smooth as you planned. That's why I don't understand your salty mood."

"I'm a chef. I'm allowed to be temperamental." Jake swung the kitchen door forward with more energy than necessary and headed toward his office. He stopped short at an elaborate display of small sculptures made from oranges. "What is this?"

Vinnie picked up one of the orange carvings. "Nice, isn't it."

"Whose idea was this, anyway?"

"One of the kitchen crew heard how ballerinas eat oranges for energy. His friend in the Thai restaurant down the street showed him how to make swans and baskets." He popped an orange slice into his mouth. "Not a bad orange for this time of the year."

Jake replied with a grunt and continued to the sanctuary of his office.

Vinnie followed. "I think ya need to talk?"

"Don't you have more important things to do than dole out advice to me. We've got a busy day scheduled."

"S'matter with ya?" Vinnie flung his hands in the air.

"First ya add too many eggs to your soufflé. Ya beat up the cream. But ya liked the oranges. Didn't ya?"

"The oranges are a nice touch."

"Things work out okay between ya and the ballerina?"

"What things are you referring to?" Jake asked.

"Just things." Vinnie shrugged. His attempt to coax Jake into a better mood was in vain. "Fine, I'll let you marinade in your misery. I've got a lot to do." Vinnie strutted back to the kitchen. Over his shoulder he said, "Ya gotta be at the bridge in a half hour."

Jake slammed the door to his office. He knew very well where he had to be. How would Rebecca act when she saw him? Jake had been brewing over it all morning. Memories of the previous evening cluttered his mind. He had almost tossed Antonio's citrus glaze across the kitchen. When the unsuspecting chef added neroli oil, the resulting orange fragrance permeated the air. All night Jake had tossed and turned, remembering the sweetness of Rebecca's kiss.

Rebecca glanced at her watch as she hurried up the stairs into the fresh air. After being crammed into the crowded subway she was sorry she hadn't accepted Les's offer to pick her up. She was glad to be leaving the dingy train behind. She took a deep breath and studied her surroundings. The span of the bridge was directly across the street. She wondered how far onto the bridge the camera crew had set up.

At the midway point between Manhattan and Brooklyn Rebecca found the group. In the small narrow walkway a crowd had gathered. She edged her way through the crowd. Everyone in the crowd hoped they would catch a glimpse of someone famous. Above the heads of the people she spotted a tall chef's hat. Jake had said he would be there attired in his grandest apparel. Her own costume had been picked up earlier by a messenger and delivered to the set before dawn.

When she reached the roped-off area, Jake was engrossed in a conversation with one of the spectators. If not for his tunic and hat, he could be mistaken for a model for an outdoor catalog. She was disappointed he didn't notice her arrival. But Les did.

"Hurry up, Becky. The people from the newspaper want to do individual interviews." Les placed his arm around her waist and ushered her into a changing tent.

A cool breeze fluttered the canvas door flap giving Rebecca a view of the activities around her makeshift changing room. Jake must have been doing his interview. An attractive young girl with a pen and pad attentively jotted down his every word.

"If you would get someone to help me into my tutu I'll be out in a flash." With a gentle shove she pushed Les out.

An assistant helped her slip into a vivid red costume. Layers of stiff tulle attached to a jeweled bodice. From the top of her bun to tips of her ruby slippers she was transformed into an elegant ballerina. She parted the canvas. With caution she stepped out onto her gray concrete stage. The oohs and aahs from the crowd acknowledged her transformation.

Against a backdrop of steel cables Jake and Les were being positioned by the photographer. She accepted the hands they offered and glided into position between them.

"I just love the ballet." A woman in the crowd sighed. "It's so lovely."

"Don't get emotional, lady," the man next to her said. "They're just filming a commercial."

"What kinda commercial?"

"For one of them new cars."

"I don't see a car."

"They put it in later."

Rebecca listened to the comments from the crowd. Everyone had an opinion as to why the chef, the ballerina, and the man in a suit performed for the cameras. No one came close to the real reason.

Rebecca would do anything to help Lilliana save the school. After being around Jake and Les, she knew they weren't as committed to Lilliana as she was. Jake's involvement was more for the old neighborhood than a specific cause. And Les, she wasn't sure of. She wanted to believe he had a change of heart because of their friendship, but knew he was most likely trying to show up Jake Fleichman.

"Let's see some moves from the dancer." The photographer looked through his camera lens.

Jake stood frozen in position. As hard as he tried, he couldn't find the words to describe the lovely creature beside him. Her red tutu added an air of enchantment to the worn bricks and weathered steel that suspended the bridge over the churning East River. He wanted to take her in his arms. He could almost feel the silky sensation of the jeweled bodice beneath his fingers.

Distracted by the sound of a horn, Jake glanced at the river below. A lone tug moved upstream. Like the little boat pulling the barge, Jake would have to push against the currents of his past if he wanted to continue seeing Rebecca. In the brief second he had looked away, the photographer had started shooting.

"This is great." The photographer seized the opportunity. He moved closer, focusing his lens on Rebecca and Les.

"Wonderful. Respond to her," he instructed Les. The camera kept clicking.

Les stepped beside Rebecca. She stood on her toes. With little tiny steps she fluttered away, while she shook a scolding finger at him. Les pressed his palms together and issued a silent plea even Jake understood. He asked for her forgiveness. Even thought he was envious that Les had gotten to Rebecca first, Jake was beginning to understand Les's attraction to the ballet. If she asked for the world, he would hand it to her on a silver platter.

"Out of film," the camera man announced. "Take five."

"Isn't the ballet enchanting, Fleichman?" Les stepped back with admiration and affection in his eyes.

Although Rebecca stood away from the men, they both watched her. She bent down to adjust the tie on her slipper, unaware she was their topic of conversation.

"I've never seen anything more inviting." Jake leaned against the rail with his arms folded across his chest.

"Give me some more of that." The photographer reloaded his camera. "This time with the chef."

Jake took a deep breath. It was his turn. Rebecca was enjoying herself. She was doing what she loved to do. The crowd had grown larger. Women with shopping bags stood alongside rollerbladers. Jake hated to admit it, but she had him in the palm of her hand and the crowd was on her side.

Rebecca rose on her toes. Her right arm glided in the air. She turned to face him. With both hands she cradled her heart and her head inclined slightly to the left in his direction. This time her lids fluttered in rapid coy movements. Her features became more animated. It looked so easy, she must have danced this scene so many times before. Jake understood immediately: she offered him her heart.

So light on her feet, she looked as if she was suspended

in air. Like a tin soldier he was frozen in place. Afraid to react.

But Rebecca's invitation was a challenge he found hard to resist. He held out his hand. She accepted. He moved toward her, driven involuntarily by his own desire. She swung weightless into his arms. He pressed his lips to hers then released her and stepped aside. In one sweeping motion he removed his hat, bent at the waist, and acknowledged his public with a gallant bow. The crowd loved their pantomime. They went wild with applause.

At first he thought his kiss threw off her balance. Not to be upstaged, she glided into a low graceful bow.

"You kids were great. Let's call it a day." The photographer had taken his last shot. "Got a minute, Fleichman?"

Rebecca rushed off in the direction of her dressing room. Les stepped in front of her. "Another wonderful performance." He clapped his hands together in a slow, repetitious beat. "It seems Flechiman has learned a thing or two from you," he said with a twinge of envy.

"He's actually quite a showman." She didn't want to make Les feel bad. "You did pretty well yourself."

"I meant what I said before." Les showed her his open palms in a gesture of peace. "I never had any intention of throwing Lilliana out onto the street. I could have started proceedings months ago."

"Then why cause all this commotion?"

"When Lilliana brought Fleichman into the picture, I was a little annoyed at first. Then I realized I couldn't resist the challenge."

"All this is a game to you?"

"Don't kid yourself, one of Fleichman's favorite pastimes is trying to outsmart me too."

"Why?" She searched his face for an explanation.

"Just something we had going on since we were kids."

"Anything to do with the townhouse?" Rebecca realized she knew very little about Jake. "I saw it last night."

"Nice, isn't it?" Les shrugged. "I could have made a fortune with that property."

"You mean your constant bickering and trying to outdo each other is not about losing the sale to Jake."

"Your knight in shining armor is no angel." Les chuckled. "He likes this friendly bantering too."

Rebecca felt silly standing on the Brooklyn Bridge in a bright red tutu trying to coax information out of her friend. She was thankful to the group of fans who rushed toward her for autographs, but she really needed to break away. She didn't want Jake to leave before she had a chance to speak to him.

In her makeshift tent she slipped out of her tutu and put her jeans on over her leotard. When Rebecca exited the crew was packing their equipment into a golf cart. The crowd had dispersed. Les was busy with the reporter. She didn't see Jake.

"You were unbelievable." He came up behind her unexpectedly. The flap of his chef's tunic was unbuttoned. "Which way are you walking?"

"You weren't so bad yourself," she said. "I'm going to catch a cab on the Manhattan side."

"Mind if I walk with you?"

"Do you have the time?"

"I've got all the time I need. Everything is set for this evening." Hoping to avoid her irresistible dark eyes, Jake looked out over the river. "All we have to do is get dressed and greet our guests."

"I hope everything works out as planned." There was an edge of doubt in her voice.

"Believe me, I've done this before." He hadn't offered to walk across the bridge to discuss the benefit. He wanted to tell her he had spent a miserable night and equally miserable morning. It wasn't until he saw her on the bridge that his day and mood improved. More important, he wanted to explain about last evening.

They had left the bridge behind and were walking toward the concrete canyons of Wall Street. Jake reached for her arm. "Rebecca, stop. We've got to talk about yesterday."

"I had a wonderful time. So did your daughter." Her eyes narrowed suspiciously. "Didn't you?"

"It was not my usual market day," he confessed.

"You mean you don't usually juggle fruits and vegetables, or . . ." her voice lowered to a whisper, "kiss your business partner?"

"I was trying to honor your conditions for our working relationship. I thought it was a good idea to keep our association strictly business." He couldn't tell her that it was also strong protection from her alluring eyes that burned through his soul and cracked the protective wall around his heart.

"I believe we crossed the line last night," Rebecca said.

He took her hands. "Maybe we didn't."

"You mean we didn't really kiss." She appeared amused by his answer.

He had gone over this scenario so many times he thought it would be easy for her to understand. "I thought maybe what we felt was our passion for the event."

"Let me see if I've got this straight." There was no humor in her tone. "You kissed me the way you did because you were excited about tonight's party."

"Sometimes people confuse their enthusiasm with their feelings. After tonight we'll return to our old lives." He refused to look into her eyes. "We live in different worlds." He had no intention of falling under her spell. "I never go to the ballet and you barely eat." He could feel the knot wrenching in his gut. "What will we have in common after all this is over?" he lied.

Rebecca's face showed no expression. Jake had become accustomed to reading her thoughts through her gestures. The blank stare she affixed on him sent a shiver through his body.

"I didn't know psychiatry was on your menu." She stepped closer, barely touching him. "What about the little scene on the bridge? I know you got my meaning."

He could feel his defenses melting, but she still aroused old fears and uncertainties. "Becky, listen to me." He realized he had used her childhood name. "It was play-acting. Just like that day in the deli. You're very good at what you do."

"Thank you." Her eyes teased him but her voice sounded a little too acid. "And what is it I do so well?"

"You dazzle your audience. You throw stardust into their eyes. I can't ask you to give all that up." His little speech wasn't very convincing. If it had been, he wouldn't be standing here trying to think of a thousand reasons not to take her in his arms.

"Shouldn't that be my decision?"

"Are you ready to make the choice?" He needed a distraction before he began apologizing for the stupid things he tried to say. As if conjured by his thoughts, an empty cab cruised by. Jake waved his hand in the air. "Taxi." He hailed the driver. "We'll talk more later. You better go. You know how difficult it is to get a cab down here."

Just before the taxicab pulled away Rebecca rolled down the window. "Are you sure everything is in order for tonight?"

"Absolutely," he assured her.

Chapter Nine

Jake knew every beat to the pulse of his restaurant. By a simple break in the rhythm he could detect anxious staff, unhappy customers, or equipment malfunctions. As soon as Jake walked through the open door he knew something was out of order. The scene that greeted him shouted malfunction. The dining room was too quiet. Windows and doors were wedged open. Waiters cooled themselves with menus and other makeshift fans.

"What happened?" Jake scanned the dining room.

A young waiter rushed forward with the bad news. "The air conditioner broke, boss."

In the kitchen the staff had stripped down to T-shirts. The door to the back alley was open and huge fans had been placed strategically in the far corners. However, his army had not deserted their posts. Frying pans sizzled and pots of boiling water sent steam flowing into the already overheated air. In spite of the heat, his kitchen staff assured him dinner would be served on time.

"Where's Vinnie?" Jake asked.

"Out in the alley. Checking the a.c."

Jake found Vinnie hunched over the main unit, shirt sleeves rolled up and a wrench in his back pocket. "Just like I thought." Vinnie surfaced with a black cylinder in his hand. "Hi, boss. We had a brownout earlier, but the air never clicked back on."

"It's hot out here. Unusually warm so early in June." Jake wiped the sweat from his brow. "Can it be fixed?"

"Simple. Just need to replace a burnt-out fuse."

Jake took the fuse from Vinnie. "It may not be as simple as you say. It's a Friday night. Where do you intend to find a new fuse?"

"No problem, boss. I already called my Uncle Tony."

"Can he get the job done?"

"The man has electrical contracts with almost every church in Brooklyn." Vinnie raised his eyes to the sky. "Never disappointed a customer yet. He's on his way with the new part."

"Great. Pay him whatever he asks."

"Actually, when he heard it was for the Bridge Cafe he asked for a reservation as payment."

"Book him this weekend. It's on the house."

"No need. I couldn't find a spot for him until September so I told him to bring along a suit. Okay if he stays for the party?"

"I don't care if he brings the entire Vatican, as long as he fixes the air."

"Maybe not the Pope, but close to it. He's bringing my aunt and the girls."

"Do the girls include your infamous cousin Vivian?"

"Not to worry, my matchmaking attempts for you are over." Vinnie looked over Jake's shoulder. "Where's the ballerina?"

"She went home to change." Jake looked at his watch. "She'll be here about six."

"How'd the photo shoot go?"

"Fine," Jake said.

"How was that creep Morgan?"

"He was almost gracious. I don't know what Morgan has up his sleeve, but the publicity'll be good for Lilliana." Jake laughed.

"What's so funny."

"I can't believe Morgan understands all that ballet stuff." Jake brought his hands up to his heart. He tried to mimic Rebecca's gestures. "Do you know what that means?"

Vinnie scratched his head. "No. Should I?"

"Morgan understood every move Rebecca made. Every step she took. Every look she gave him." Jake's voice drifted off into a whisper.

"What'd ya do?"

"I played the crowd." Jake bowed at the waist. "I must have gotten the correct message. The crowd loved it."

"What ya two guys doing?" Uncle Tony had arrived. He held a navy blue suit in one hand and a fuse in the other. "Nice place ya got here."

Jake took off his chef's jacket. Sweat rolled into his eyes. He removed a handkerchief from his pocket and tied it around his forehead. It took all three of them to twist the rusty cover loose.

"Watch the sharp edge," Uncle Tony warned.

Jake twisted his wrist to glance at his watch. Rebecca and Jewel would be arriving soon. Uncle Tony's warning came too late. A stray piece of metal sliced across Jake's forearm.

"Ya should wash off that cut before ya get an infection," Uncle Tony instructed in a heavy Brooklyn accent.

Jake took his advice and went in to clean his wound. He returned with three frosty long necks.

The job was completed in record time. The welcome hum of the working air conditioner brought a hearty cheer from the kitchen. Jake, Vinnie, and Uncle Tony had time to share a cold beer. Sitting on the steps to the back door was the most relaxed Jake had felt in days. Just three guys from the neighborhood talking about old times. That's where they were when Rebecca arrived. Mrs. Lopez dropped off Jewel at the same time.

"Que bella!" Uncle Tony was the first to notice the ladies.

Jake couldn't have expressed it better. He had thought Rebecca looked great in jeans and sensational in a leotard. Tonight she looked delectable. It wasn't just the way her dress swayed around her legs, or her warm smile that greeted the sweaty men. Tonight she wore her hair loose. Jake had never seen her with her hair down.

"Hi." She turned her head to greet everyone. Long soft curls fell across her shoulders. Raven wisps brushed over her face when she moved her head. Tempted to brush them off her cheek, Jake had to restrain himself. He folded his arms across his chest.

However, Uncle Tony showed more familiarity and brushed the black curls with the back of his hand. "Who are these beautiful ladies?"

Jewel giggled. "You mean a lady and a kid." She twirled, the hem of her pale blue dress flaring in a perfect circle.

"This lovely little lady is my daughter Jewel." Jake took

his daughter's hand. "And this lovely lady is my associate, Rebecca Carr."

"Pleased to meet ya." Uncle Tony looked Rebecca over from head to toe. He nodded his approval. Then with a raised brow turned to his nephew. "His associate?"

"Don't ask." Vinnie ushered his uncle inside. "Come on, Jewel."

Rebecca and Jake stood alone among the trash cans and brick walls. Even in the drab alleyway her eyes sparkled. She looked like she had fallen from a star. He remembered a story he had read to Jewel, a Russian fairy tale adapted for the ballet. Jewel loved the tale about the magical bird. If Rebecca had been dressed in red, Jake would believe her to be the enchanted firebird. But she would need no magic feather to enchant him.

"We'll have to talk later," he said.

"Later will be fine." Rebecca wrinkled her nose. "You can't greet your guests looking like this."

He looked at the grease stains on his pants. "People should start arriving in a couple of hours. I'm going to run home to shower and change."

"Will you be back in time?" There was a hint of anxiety in her voice.

"You don't need me for this part." He kissed the top of her head lingering long enough to inhale the citrus scent of her shampoo. "You know, I've never seen your hair down. You should wear it that way more often."

Rebecca didn't know what to think of him. His departing kiss showed more gratitude than passion. Just a few hours ago he was trying to convince her how wrong they were for each other. After tonight there would be little reason for them to see each other again. At least that's what Jake had tried to tell her.

Inside the restaurant Rebecca noticed that everyone had a chore. Busboys and waiters were busy setting up the buffet stations. The kitchen crew placed elaborate hors d'oeuvres on silver trays.

She declined their offers to sample the delicacies. "I couldn't possibly start eating so early."

Jake's grandparents were the first to arrive. They greeted Rebecca with an affectionate kiss but were anxious for a look behind the scenes. "We better go see what those boys are doing in the kitchen." They disappeared.

More guests began to trickle in. She wished Jake would show up soon. Finally a familiar face. On the arm of a distinguished man Lilliana made her entrance. Rebecca hadn't seen Dave Burke since his wife's death. He had aged considerably. But there was something bright in his eyes as he ushered Lilliana into the room. They greeted her and rushed off to mix with the other guests.

The main dining room started to bustle with activity. The kitchen staff had donned their best attire. In crisp tunics and black and white baggy pants they served egg rolls from Jenny Lu's in Sunset Park, alongside Russian foods from Brighton Beach and stuffed grape leaves from Atlantic Avenue.

"So you're really a ballerina." The man standing next to her reached for a glass of champagne. He handed Rebecca one too.

She accepted the glass, took a sip, then handed it to a passing waiter.

A small group had gathered around them. The questions were always the same. "How do you stay on your toes so long? When can my daughter start pointe? Did you always want to be a ballerina?"

Rebecca kept looking from the main entrance to the

swinging kitchen doors. She hoped nothing had happened to Jake.

Vinnie must have noticed her concern. "Don't worry, he'll be here soon." He handed her a glass of champagne, reassured her, and rushed off to supervise the busboys.

Perhaps she expected Jake to arrive in a starched tunic and tall chef's hat. The man who stepped from the shadow of the entry took her breath away. The simple but elegant cut of his tuxedo made him look like one of the affluent guests.

"Where have you been?" Rebecca reached out and clutched his arm. Through the expensive fabric, strong hard muscles teased her fingertips.

"You seem to have everything under control." He smiled warmly and looked down at her empty glass. "I wanted to look my best."

"You look fine." She brushed an imaginary spec off his sleeve.

He placed his hand over hers. He smiled almost apologetically. "Let's see how things are going in the kitchen." Jake led her around the little clusters of guests.

He shook hands with a man who rushed up to give him a compliment. "Most innovative chef in New York."

Rebecca smiled, but didn't really hear the man's name. Something about being president of a local cable network. Her attention was elsewhere.

In a secluded corner Rebecca spotted Lilliana and Dave sitting alone at a small table. With their arms linked they sipped champagne from each other's glasses. She looked away quickly to avoid being caught spying on the intimate scene.

Jake must have noticed the romantic encounter too. "So Lilliana and Mr. Wall Street really did have a thing years ago?" He patted her hand. "They have you to thank for bringing them together again. You're a real matchmaker." He held the kitchen door open, allowing Rebecca entry to the secrets of tonight's success.

Greeting each member of the crew, Jake asked questions about spices, cooking times, and servers. He tasted and offered some suggestions.

When Jake slipped out the back door she knew he was going to check the air conditioning unit. The evening could take a disastrous turn if their guests started to sweat in their expensive clothes. The weather was unseasonably hot for the beginning of summer.

Rebecca decided not to follow Jake out into the humid night air. She could have returned to the party but the behind-the-scenes preparations fascinated her. She watched a sous chef as he carved a turkey. With an elongated knife he sliced through the joint connecting the thigh to the body. When he was done he placed each slice back on the frame. She waited, expecting him to re-feather the roasted bird. Instead, he placed garnishes of bright summer vegetables around the platter.

"Everything appears to be in working order." Jake had stepped behind her. He picked up a slice of turkey meat that hadn't made it back onto the bird and put it in his mouth. "Perfect."

"I didn't think he missed a slice," Rebecca said.

"Amazing, isn't it. The man is a true artist."

The chef took a bow and rushed off to work on his next creation. At another counter, two of the kitchen crew were busy cutting the meat off a pig. Piles of fresh roasted pork rested in a ring of lemon and lime slices.

"Did you roast that here?" Rebecca asked.

"Not this guy. He was wrapped in leaves and roasted in

a hole in the ground. There's a great Puerto Rican caterer on Eighteenth Avenue. He roasts these pigs right in his back yard." Jake pulled off a shred of tender pork and handed it to Rebecca. "Taste it. You'll want more."

Rebecca nodded her approval. The meat tasted tender and sweet.

"Let's move it to the plates," Jake commanded.

Trays laden with moussaka, pastrami, and poached fish purchased fresh off the boats in Sheepshead Bay joined the procession behind the roasted turkey and pig. Jake and Rebecca followed the scent of cumin, capers, and citrus into the dining room.

The lights dimmed as they circled the crowd, teasing their senses with the smells and vision of their favorite foods.

"What's going on?" Jake pulled Vinnie off to the side.

"The dim lights were a nice touch." Rebecca looked from Jake to Vinnie. She felt their uneasiness. "That wasn't supposed to happen?"

"Everyone in the city is probably turning on their air conditioning for the first time. Con Ed can't handle it." Jake tried to sound reassuring. "Let's join the party." He put his hand on her elbow and ushered her over to the small group seated at a corner table.

Dave Burke stood up and offered Rebecca his seat. "Great party, Fleichman." He put his arm around Jake's shoulder. "The man is one of the most fearless chefs I ever met. Look at this combination of great foods. All these people popping antacid. Pharmaceutical stocks will soar tomorrow." When Dave laughed he seemed ten years younger.

"Be careful what you say. You'll send everyone running

out to call their broker." Jake shook hands with the Wall Street Iron Man. "Nice to see you again."

"It's time I started getting out again," Dave's voice cracked. Regaining his composure he glanced at Lilliana. "I wish Lil had called me when she realized she was in trouble."

"And what would you have done?" Lilliana looked past Dave and her expression turned sour. "Here he comes now. The big shot landlord."

Rebecca realized she must have been in the kitchen when Les arrived. He had promised he would behave tonight but Lilliana had a way of sparking his wrath. A waiter passed with a tray of champagne. Rebecca reached for two glasses. She sipped from one and handed the other to Lilliana.

Les greeted the group. He was very cordial to Lilliana when he realized Dave Burke was her escort. "Did Becky tell you about the piece the *News* is doing on us?"

"No, she didn't," Lilliana said.

"Jake, Les, and I took some photos on the bridge this morning. There's going to be an article about the school in the Sunday paper," Rebecca explained.

"And you forgot to tell me this." There was a hint of disappointment in Lilliana's voice.

Rebecca sighed. Of all people, she looked to Jake for help but he seemed preoccupied with his own thoughts and hadn't heard the last part of the conversation. "We just found out yesterday. I'm surprised we all managed to get here on time."

"I know how Lilliana feels," Les interrupted. "You've been so busy you haven't had much time for your old friends. You never told me there was going to be an auction tonight."

"I didn't think you'd be interested in bidding on wine."

"You're right, it's not the wine I'm going to be bidding on."

"Les, you can't do that." Rebecca wanted to tell him not to bid against Jake. At that moment Bubbe joined their little group. In each hand she balanced a plate overflowing with food. Rebecca was glad for the interruption. Trying to convince Les not to join the bidding would be futile. He would never give up the chance to challenge Jake. She would be the innocent pawn in their ongoing battle.

"You two better eat." Bubbe took Rebecca's empty glass. She placed it on the table and handed her a plate full of food.

Jake took the other plate, glanced at it, then passed it over to Les. "Here, enjoy yourself. I've got to check something."

Ever since the lights dimmed earlier Jake had been preoccupied. Rebecca sat down at the table across from Les. She tasted a small bite of each food.

"You going to eat the mozzarella?" Les didn't wait for her to answer. He jabbed the marinated cheese ball with his fork and moved it to his plate. "That Fleichman is a great cook."

"He's not a cook." Rebecca felt a need to defend Jake. "He's a chef."

"Did you know his ex-wife was a chef too?" Les offered.

"No, I didn't." She watched Les continue to stuff his face. This morning Jake had tried to convince her they were wrong for each other. They had nothing in common. Their feelings toward each other would pass when the party was over. But if similar interests were so important to him, why did his marriage fail?

Rebecca cupped the empty glass in her hand. She exchanged it for a full one. Over the rim she watched as the lights flickered on and off.

"Oops. Too much power being used." Les took a sip from her glass. "Always happens during these unexpected heat waves. You'd think Con Ed could avoid these brownouts."

"I hope the lights don't go out." Rebecca giggled. It must have been the champagne, because there was nothing funny about about a potential blackout.

"I'm sure your boyfriend has an emergency generator."

"I hope so." She searched the crowded dining room, hoping to find Jake busy entertaining his guests and not out checking the electricity.

"Sweaty palms can't write big checks." Les stood up and patted his stomach. "Let's see what else I can get for my hefty donation." He joined the line at the bar. The decor had been converted into an old-fashioned candy store. Lilliana and Dave stood at the bar. They sipped from wide-lipped glasses filled with frothy egg creams.

Rebecca spotted Vinnie and headed in his direction. "Is everything okay? I haven't seen Jake in a while."

"He's giving his final approval to the desserts." There was something unconvincing about Vinnie's answer.

None of the other guests seemed to notice the lights had dimmed again. The auctioneer had taken his place at the podium. Rebecca followed the crowd. The man next to her offered her a list of the items to be auctioned. At the top of the list were Jake's favorite wines, followed by a meal for ten cooked by the celebrated Jake Fleichman. Fortunately a date with the City Ballet's prima ballerina was last on the list. By then Jake should have handled his crisis and be available to bid.

The bidding for the wine went fast. Lilliana rushed over

to hug Rebecca. The older woman mumbled something about a six-figure donation before she hurried off to share the good news with Dave.

"And now the best for last." The auctioneer offered Rebecca his hand.

She accepted the barstool Vinnie positioned near the podium. A date with Vinnie had been sold to the charming wife of the man who won the dinner. Her husband, a portly little man whose belt couldn't find his nonexistent waist, opened the bid for Rebecca.

Numbers started to roll off the auctioneer's tongue. "Two hundred, two hundred. Do I hear two-fifty?" He pointed to Les Morgan. "Two-fifty, do I hear three hundred?"

The bids were flowing so fast Rebecca believed the bidders was bidding against themselves. Why didn't Jake chime in?

"Five hundred from the big spender tonight. Five hundred, do I hear five-fifty?"

"Five hundred and fifty from the man in front." Again he pointed to Les. "Do I hear six hundred for a date with this elegant ballerina?"

Rebecca held her breath. Silently she prayed for Jake to outbid Les. Over the crowd she saw him. Jake leaned casually against the back wall. "Six hundred," he said.

"Six hundred, do I hear six-fifty?" With his gavel raised in the air the auctioneer prepared for his final call. Six hundred once, six hundred—"

At that very moment the lights in the restaurant and all of New York City went off.

"Six hundred twice." The gravel hit the podium. "Sold for six hundred dollars to our host for the evening."

Chapter Ten

Emergency generators kicked on minutes after the room went dark. The audience, too content with drink and food, hardly noticed the short disturbance. They applauded the auctioneer's perseverance.

When the lights came on, Jake walked up to claim his prize. "This was one time I knew I'd win," he said as he walked past Morgan.

"You win some, you lose some." Les shrugged. "You were lucky the lights went off just in time."

Rebecca was not about to become a new issue for them to dispute. She jumped off the podium and rushed over to where the men stood. They both reached for her, but it was Jake's arm that glided around her waist.

"So we've got a date." He planted a light kiss on her cheek. "I hate to run but I've got to check on the air conditioner." With an obvious edge of sarcasm Jake said to Les, "You wouldn't mind escorting the lady to the dessert tables, would you?"

"It would be my pleasure." Les's hand replaced Jake's along the small of her back. He must have felt her tense and tried to reassure her. "Everything is going great."

"Is it?" Rebecca heard herself reply.

"Sure, I spoke to the Mayor this evening. He thinks the school building can be designated a landmark."

"Sounds like a good idea." Although she heard every word Les said, her mind was wandering. She was thinking about her date with Jake. Where would they go? What would they do?

"Hey Becky, are you with me?" Les snapped his fingers in front of her face.

"I heard you. You're going to save the building from demolition. Jake will be pleased."

"Why don't you go find him and tell him the good news," Les suggested.

The dinner stations were being cleared to make way for dessert. Around the bar the candy store was busy. Waiters served large colorful lollipops, jelly apples, and cotton candy.

Jewel was closely supervising the placement of each sweet. She had kept a low profile for most of the evening.

"Where have you been?" Rebecca asked.

"Bubbe told me not to bother the adults."

"Have you seen your dad?"

"Are you looking for him?" Jewel asked. Rebecca had seen that mischievous twinkle in Jewel's eyes before. "He's looking for you too. He said something about asking you to join him on the patio out back."

"He told you all this?" Rebecca didn't want to doubt the

child's word. If Jake wanted to see her in private it must be important. She shouldn't keep him waiting. "Where is this patio?"

"Just past Dad's office." Jewel reached for two glasses of champagne. "Take these."

Before Rebecca could reach for the glasses Jewel's hands stopped in mid air. "What do ya think you're doing with those?" Vinnie looked down at the child.

"Hi, Uncle Vinnie." Jewel smiled. "They're not for me."

"Who they for?" Vinnie's tone was stern.

"Dad and Miss Becky." Did the child just wink at Vinnie?

"Why can't they get their own drinks?"

Jewel let out a big sigh. "Because Miss Becky is going to meet Dad on the patio." The child continued in a low tone. She paused after each word. "Don't you remember, Dad asked us to send her out there."

"What ya talking about?" Vinnie seemed confused. "Your dad's in his office."

"Great." Jewel handed the glasses to Rebecca, then gently urged Vinnie in the direction of Jake's office. "Tell him we found Miss Becky and she's waiting on the patio."

"Oh, okay, I'll do that." Vinnie had the same naughty look as Jewel.

Before meeting Jake on the patio, Rebecca had to make an urgent detour to the ladies room. "Too much champagne," she said aloud. She placed the glasses on a ledge and entered the restroom. Luckily there was no line. She walked into the first empty stall.

Rebecca didn't intend to eavesdrop on the conversation at the sink. There was no place for her to go without embarrassing the women or herself.

"Isn't that Jake Fleichman the perfect man," the first voice said.

"Too bad they didn't put him on the auction block." The next voice mixed with the hum of the hand dryer. "There wasn't a woman in the room who wouldn't have bid for a date with him."

"But who could compete with that adorable ballerina." The woman sighed. "Like the song says, everything's beautiful at the ballet."

"Did you see the way he looked at her from across the room?" Purses clicked shut. "He never took his eyes off of her." The hand dryer shut off. "Do you think she was aware he watched her every move?" The door banged announcing their departure.

Rebecca was free to leave the confines of her stall. She studied her reflection in the mirror. She wished she had brought her evening bag with her. Her lips could use a touch up. With her fingers she fluffed her hair. "This will have to do."

Jake waited on the empty patio. He pinched a purple flower from an overflowing basil plant. The sharp scent lingered on his fingers. Around the brick wall bright lanterns glowed with emergency power, supplied by several back-up generators. At the Bridge Cafe it was business as usual. Candles burned in the windows of the adjoining buildings. Except for the occasional hum of a generator, the city was silent and dark.

Within seconds after the blackout, all the city officials at the party converged in Jake's office. Before leaving, the Mayor assured them this little inconvience was only temporary.

"It's bright out here." Rebecca stepped from the shadows of the dark alley. "Jewel said you wanted to speak to me."

"That's funny." Jake took the glasses she held and placed them on the table behind him. "Vinnie said you wanted to speak to me." He held up a just-opened bottle of Dom Perignon. "Handed me this bottle as I walked out."

"I had a feeling those two were up to something. This is lovely," Rebecca said. She twirled in a circle surveying the little brick enclave. "I never imagined anything this nice could be hidden back here."

"This is the Brooklyn you never knew," Jake teased. "Actually we use this for small private parties if the weather permits."

"It's perfect out here tonight." Rebecca took several sips of the champagne. She stepped back, using the table to steady herself.

Jake reacted on impulse when he slipped his arm around her waist. He took the glass from her and placed it on the table.

"I'm fine. Too much champagne on an empty stomach." In a clumsy move Rebecca sat on the chair Jake positioned beneath her.

"How much did you have?"

"I started a glass or two, or was it three. I don't think I finished them." She giggled. "Did we decide why we're out here?"

"I think we did." He regarded the usually in control Miss Carr with amusement. "Jewel and Vinnie seemed to think we needed to talk."

"I agree. Now that we're here I have something to tell you." She placed her elbows on the table and leaned toward him. "You are not as perfect as the ladies in the bathroom said."

"Oh, I'm not?" Jake decided to play along. He was enjoying the candor the champagne brought out.

"No. You are a liar. Not a bad liar." She stood up and walked in a small circle around the table, her eyes never leaving his face.

"I didn't know there were bad liars and good liars."

"All liars are bad." She shook her finger at him. "You should never lie. Even to yourself."

"You think I lie to myself." Jake didn't want to admit she was right on target. He had a bank of excuses. His family, his business, his daughter, a million alibis justifying his reasons to avoid a permanent relationship. He was prepared to hold onto those excuses forever. Until Rebecca appeared and shattered his reasoning.

"Absolutely. You don't allow yourself to have what you really want. Then you lie to everyone and say you didn't want it anyway."

Jake stepped closer, capturing her between the table and the chair. "What is it you think I want."

They stood disturbingly close but Jake couldn't pull himself away.

"Right now you'd probably like to kiss me." She put her hands on his chest.

"The thought had crossed my mind." Jake leaned closer.

"Go ahead and try." She shook her head. Her hair fell around her shoulders. "It won't hurt."

He twisted his fingers in her hair. "Are you changing the rules? You do remember the rules, don't you? No pleasure. Just business."

"We changed the rules last night. I don't believe that nonsense about confusing our feelings."

Jake sat down gently nudging the table. Rebecca had placed her unfinished champagne too close to the edge. His strong fingers closed around the delicate stem just in time to prevent a disaster. In one gulp he finished the remaining champagne and poured some more. Maybe he needed a dose of what she was drinking so he could share her honesty.

"I'm afraid the truth will get me in trouble." Jake had listened to what she had to say. Now it was his turn. "I'm not ready to handle trouble."

"Or the truth," Rebecca said.

There was a painful place inside him that no woman had been able to find. As hard as they tried, he managed to keep it hidden. Somehow, Rebecca had healed some of the scarring. He had to be sure it was for the right reasons.

"There's a room full of men out there who would give anything to be in my place right now." Leaning forward in his chair, Jake choose his words carefully. He reached across the small table and closed his hands over hers. "Some of them might even lie just to tell you what you want to hear." He took another sip and passed the glass to Rebecca.

"No thanks. I've already had too much." She fanned herself with open hands.

With his hands clasped behind his head Jake leaned back in his chair. He knew she understood what he was telling her. He was glad she didn't challenge him. The evening had already taken its share of unexpected twists and turns. He gave her the floor. "I'm anxious to hear what other words of wisdom you overheard in the ladies room."

"I'm sure you already know the auction was a huge success." She looked at him from the corner of her eye. "The ladies were surprised you weren't on the auction block."

"Would you have bid for me?"

Rebecca didn't answer right away. "I couldn't leave you

to the mercy of the crowd." Her cheeks were red. He wasn't sure if it was the champagne, the warm evening air, or if he had truly put her on the spot.

"Are you happy with the way things went this evening?" Jake asked.

"Why shouldn't I be?" Rebecca's tone had changed from playful and giddy to serious. "Les gets his money, Lilliana gets to keep her school, and your critics give you rave reviews."

Her eyes tore at his heart. He stood up, then pulled her to her feet. "What about you, Becky? What did you get?"

"I guess time will answer that for me." She shrugged her shoulders. "I'm just happy things worked out so well for everyone. Whatever I found was a bonus." Her lips brushed against his cheek.

"We better get back to the party." He forced himself to step back.

"You're right, our guests are waiting. There's still more to come before the final curtain call." She turned and walked back to toward the restaurant.

Thoughts smoldered in Jake's head. Glad their conversation ended on a sober note he was also disturbed by the idea that he might never see her again. Jewel would be disappointed, his grandmother disenchanted, and Vinnie frustrated. Most of all he would want to kick himself in the morning. He took a step to follow her, when Vinnie appeared.

"There ya are, boss."

"Where did you think I'd be? You're the one who sent me out here."

"How'd it go?" Vinnie asked.

"Like the lady said, there's still more to come before the final curtain call."

"Jewel will be happy to hear things went well."

"Since when did you and my conniving daughter become a team?" Jake put his hand on Vinnie's shoulder. "Why are you looking for me?"

"That guy from the cable network's been lookin for ya."

"Know what he wants?" Jake didn't want to deal with any more issues tonight.

"Somethin' about a TV spot on 'Chef Du Jour'."

"The guy's been trying to recruit me for the last six months."

"Want me to distract him?"

"No," Jake said. "I think he might have the answer he wants." An idea occurred to him. "Bubbe and I have a special treat planned. Have him meet me at the dessert buffet."

"Ya gonna do the show?"

"I might." Jake let out a long relieved sigh. "If I can convince a certain lady to be my assistant."

Chapter Eleven

Rebecca peered over Les's shoulder. At the table, Jake's grandmother layered perfect circles of sponge cake in round cardboard holders. No master chef's attire for Bubbe. She wore a white bakery apron over her sequined gown. With great skill and care, she created a small mound of whipped cream over the cake. Her stiff fingers suddenly seemed limber and graceful. For a grand finale she placed either a candied cherry or strawberry on top of each creation.

"And that is how you make a charlotte russe." Bubbe acknowledged the applause.

"I haven't had a charlotte since I was a kid," Les said. "Let's get closer before they run out."

Rebecca stood next to Les as he inched nearer the table. She too remembered the thrill of seeing the little cakes displayed in a glass case on a bakery counter.

Jake had taken his position beside his grandmother. He handed out the paper cups faster than Bubbe could fill them. While he served, he explained the origins of these classic treats. "The charlotte russe is by no means solely from Brooklyn."

The crowd seemed disappointed to hear this bit of trivia.

Jake continued. "It was a popular Victorian dessert during the winter in city neighborhoods."

Rebecca and Les finally reached the table. Les took two charlottes and handed one to Rebecca. They watched the man next to them try vehemently to reach the cake at the bottom.

"It's the original pushup." Les demonstrated with his own cup.

Rebecca stepped off to the side to watch Jake. He had taken over the job of filling the cups, while Bubbe wrote out directions to the bakery for guests eager to sample more of her delicious breads and cakes.

Jake worked swiftly, distributing individual creations of perfection. His eyes, like those of a kid loose in a candy shop, had a mischievous glint. There was a restless energy in his movements. Rebecca watched the other women in the crowd and realized how deliciously appealing they found him. His smile made each one think it was especially for her.

Jake reached across the table and slid his finger over her bare arm. His fingers were cool from the chilled whipped cream can. "I have to speak to you," he whispered.

Rebecca opened her mouth to warn him. It was too late. With his other hand he had accidental released the nozzle on the whipped cream, leaving a trail across the table.

Immediately Bubbe wiped up the mess. "Go. Go entertain your friends." With the corner of her apron she wiped off a smudge of cream.

Jake walked around the table and stood beside Rebecca. He nodded at the creamy confection she held in her hand. "You know what a charlotte russe is?"

"Oh course I do. I grew up in Brooklyn." In spite of feeling a little insulted by the question, Rebecca couldn't help smiling. Maybe it was the memories these little cakes brought back. Simple times shopping with her parents. A time when calories didn't matter.

"Want me to show you how to eat this?" Les stepped in front of her. His upper lip was covered with cream.

Bubbe handed Les a napkin. He wiped the cream off his lip. Les and Bubbe stood side by side. Jake watched from across the table. Three sets of eyes were fixed on Rebecca.

"I know how to eat a charlotte." To prove her point she downed the strawberry and half the whipped topping in one enormous lick. "See." She waved the half-eaten cake in the air.

"Just like a true Brooklynite." Jake's lips twitched with amusement.

"You're acting like three little children standing in my bakery. Now go. I've got work to do." With the corner of her apron Bubbe scooted them away.

"Don't go far. I've got something to ask you." Jake tried to make his way around the table toward her, but well-wishers blocked his path.

Rebecca waited, anxious to hear what Jake had to say, but she found herself caught up with a similar group of guests. While Jake accepted praise and slaps on the back for a job well done, she answered questions about her up-coming season. Some of the people gathered around her were fans concerned about her injury. She assured them that she had healed well and would be back on stage that fall.

Jake's question would have to wait. She shrugged over her shoulder, hoping he wouldn't think she didn't want to hear it.

A cheer came from the already noisy dining room. News spread that the power in the city was back on. Some of the guests scurried to leave, fearing a reoccurrence. Most chose to stay. In small private circles, they lingered over coffee.

Jake was nowhere to be seen. Rebecca assumed he must have gone off to check the electricity in the kitchen.

When he reappeared Rebecca made a vain attempt to cross the room and join him, but he was accosted by Vinnie who directed him toward the bar. At the bar, Rebecca watched Jake greet a man she vaguely remembered being introduced to earlier.

Meanwhile, Rebecca found herself standing in the middle of the room, not sure which direction to go. Her first impulse was to join Jake, but he was engrossed in conversation with the man. Occasionally they both looked in her direction and smiled. It didn't seem like this was the moment to speak to Jake.

"Such a pretty lady should not be left standing alone with her thoughts." Dave Burke's warm smile reminded her of her father. He escorted her over to a table where Lilliana waited. On the way, they picked up Les. "Why don't you join us," Dave offered.

"I'm not exactly Lilliana's favorite person." Les tried to excuse himself.

"The fund raiser seems to have been very successful. You might be able to bury the hatchet." Dave put his arm around Les's shoulder. "I've got some ideas of my own I'd like to share with both of you."

Rebecca understood Les's hesitation. She knew Lilliana never liked him. However, Dave was so persuasive it was hard to refuse his invitation. She noticed the spark of interest in Les's eyes when the Iron Man expressed an interest.

Once they were all seated, Dave came right to the point. "I'd like to invite you out to the Hamptons for my annual July Fourth celebration." Dave waited while a waiter poured coffee for them. "Lil has already accepted my invitation. What about you two?"

Les didn't hesitate. "Sounds great."

"No excuses from you." Dave nodded in Rebecca's direction. "Lil's told me how you're on rest and recuperation this summer. A little break from the concrete jungle across the bridge will do you good."

"You're a hard sell. How can I refuse," Rebecca said.

"Great." Dave smiled wide with approval. "Now all we have to do is convince your boyfriend it's okay to leave his precious restaurant for a weekend."

"He's not my boyfriend."

Dave patted her hand. "It's just a figure of speech, little lady." He winked at Lilliana. "Right, Lil? Just because the man's eyes follow her across the room, why would we think there's a spark between them."

Rebecca sighed. "Jake Fleichman is a wonderful person. He was deeply committed to Lilliana's cause."

"Well then, if that's what it takes, we'll appeal to the benefactor in him." Dave waved his hand in the air. "The donations you got here tonight are a drop in the bucket, compared to what my guests will part with."

"Celebrities and big investors." Les sputtered into his coffee cup. "We don't really need Fleichman. Becky and I can appeal to the crowd at your party."

"The only thing you ever see is dollar signs." Raising a fine arched brow Rebecca scolded Les.

Lilliana jumped in to defend Jake. "This whole evening was Jake's idea. He and his crew worked hard putting this event together. They donated their time and resources so you could fill your pockets again."

"I told you I wouldn't be welcome here." Les stood up and extended his hand to Dave.

"Sit down," Dave said. "It's no secret you and Fleichman don't like each other."

Les returned to his seat. "I guess I just got carried away. It's your party; you can invite whoever you want."

"What is it you two boys have against each other?" Dave spoke to Les but looked at Rebecca. "Wouldn't have anything to do with this pretty little ballerina?"

Rebecca immediately understood Dave's presumptuous look. She felt the need to set things straight. "I just met Jake Fleichman a few weeks ago. He and Les have been battling for years."

A hearty laugh rose from Dave's chest. "I'm sure their arguments were getting stale. You have probably added a breath of fresh air to their ongoing struggle."

She knew Les wouldn't challenge Mr. Wall Street. She waited for Lilliana to come to her defense. When she didn't, Rebecca elaborated on her last statement. "Les and I have been friends forever. As I said, Jake and I only recently became involved when I realized Lil was in trouble."

"Do they remind you of anyone we knew a long time ago?" Dave directed his question to Lilliana.

"I seem to remember a young man with relentless fortitude." Lilliana smiled, but her eyes were hazy.

"And I remember a beautiful ballerina who loved her

craft more than anything else." Dave locked his fingers with Lilliana's.

Rebecca watched Dave and Lilliana. They seemed to forget they weren't alone at the table. With their eyes fixed on each other, they appeared transferred to a different place. She understood why the man was a success. She couldn't help but wonder if he had pursued Lilliana with determination. It would be rude to ask what really happened between them. Perhaps he wasn't willing to share her with her public. She knew Lilliana didn't leave the ballet until age forced her to.

"I never knew you two were old friends." Les broke the silence.

"We go way back," Lilliana said, "I knew him when he was only a tin man with an iron will."

They all laughed.

"Can anyone get in on the joke?" Jake approached the table.

He glanced at his watch. Timing was everything when serving an elaborate meal. The courses had to be perfectly spaced so the food would be served warm to people eager to eat. For the most part everything appeared effortless. When the lights went out in the city Jake instructed his crew to keep the coffee flowing.

Although he was concerned for his guests' safety, he had his own reasons for wanting to delay the end of the evening. He wanted to set things right with Rebecca. He knew he was wrong to think they had been taken in by the event. He saw it more clearly after their little rendezvous on the patio. He understood everything—especially his feelings for her.

"Pull up a chair." Dave invited him to join their group. "You're just the man I wanted to speak to."

Jake straddled a chair directly across the table from Rebecca. It amazed him how refreshed she still looked. He suddenly felt the strain of the evening. There were always unforeseen events when planning an affair of this magnitude, but the unexpected incidents this evening had taken their toll.

"You look like you could use a cup of coffee." Lilliana poured from the pot a waiter had left on the table.

Jake took a long slow sip hoping the right words would come to his mind. He was glad Dave started the conversation.

"Wasn't that guy you were talking to from one of the cable stations?" Dave asked.

"Yes, he is." Jake seized the moment. "He's offered me a spot on a cooking show."

"Great idea." Dave slapped Jake on the back. "Did you accept?"

"How could I refuse." Jake turned to Rebecca. There was no time to choose his words carefully. He would have to bring it up in front of everyone seated at the table. Maybe it would put her on the spot. She would be forced to accept his offer. It was an all-or-nothing situation.

"He'd like Rebecca to be on the show too." Jake's throat felt dry and the words seemed to get stuck. "As my assistant."

Everyone at the table agreed it was a wise decision to team them together. Everyone except Rebecca. "Me on a cooking show?"

"It's a team effort or there's no deal." Jake decided to sweeten the bait. "He's willing to let us donate any proceeds to Lilliana."

He had exaggerated the truth a little. The man was thrilled when Jake finally accepted his offer. They both agreed Rebecca would be a charming and delightful addition.

Rebecca's eyes narrowed in a frown. All other eyes at the table focused on her. Even Les was silent as they waited for her answer.

"What do you think?" Jake asked. "Would you like to do it?"

"Give the boy an answer," Dave said. "Don't leave him hanging. We've got other things to discuss."

"So we get to work together again?" There was a hopeful sparkle in her eyes. "I like the idea."

Was she wise to his little charade? Perhaps she understood him better than he thought. He hated to admit it, but he was glad he wouldn't have to play any more games.

"When will we tape?" she asked.

"Is that a yes?" He tried not to let his eagerness show.

"Will this be strictly business?" She rested her chin on her hands and smiled. "Or pleasure?"

"If you agree to assist me," Jake took a deep breath, "I'm sure it will be one of my most pleasurable cooking experiences."

"Wow, there'll be plenty of steam in that kitchen." Dave picked up his napkin and used it as a fan. "Make sure you tell us when the show airs."

"Did I miss something, or did anyone hear Becky agree to do the show with Fleichman?" Les looked around the table.

"You stay out of this, Les Morgan." Lilliana raised a scolding finger.

Rebecca stood up. With her hands on her hips, she addressed the group. "I appreciate your concern. I know you mean well, but I am capable of making my own decisions." She winked at Jake. "Jake and I will discuss this later."

"I'm sorry to bore you with all this." Jake apologized to the group. He hadn't expected everyone to offer their opinion. He hoped their advice wouldn't discourage Rebecca from making the right decision. "She's right, we'll continue our discussion later." He returned the wink. "In private."

"On the patio?" Her question was playful.

"You name the place and I'll be there." No one missed the excitement in Jake's eyes.

Dave slammed his open palms on the table. "That's settled. Now let's get down to business."

"What was it you wanted to ask me?" Jake asked.

"It seems pretty dull after all this. Just a simple party invitation," Dave said.

"An invitation to one of your parties is never dull. When is it?"

"July Fourth. My house in the Hamptons. Think you can make it?"

Jake looked at Rebecca but spoke to Dave. "I guess everyone else has already accepted your invitation?"

"They're all coming. I won't take no for an answer." It was obvious very few people ever refused an invitation from the Iron Man of Wall Street.

Jake combed his fingers through his hair. "It's a busy weekend. There'll be fireworks on the river. We're already booked solid. I'll have to let you know."

"That's what I like about you, Fleichman, no one intimidates you. Not even me." Dave offered Jake his hand. "See if you can work something out. I'd like you to be there."

"I'll see what I can do." Jake doubted he would be able to leave the restaurant on a holiday weekend.

"It's in your ballpark, little lady. See if you can use your charms to convince him." Dave gave Rebecca a fatherly kiss on the cheek. He stepped beside Lilliana and held her chair. "Ready to call it a night?"

It was ridiculous, but Jake felt a tinge of envy over Dave's kiss. When Morgan prepared to leave, Jake positioned himself in front of Rebecca so Les couldn't give her a departing kiss. Jake didn't care if his possessive maneuver annoyed Morgan.

However, Rebecca didn't let Jake's little blockade prevent her from slipping her arm through Les's. "I'll walk you out."

"Nice party, Fleichman. See you in the Hamptons." Les acknowledged Jake with a two finger salute.

Outside the restaurant, the streets were deserted. Valets scrambled for the few remaining guests' cars. The more affluent stepped into waiting limousines. Dave Burke's black town car pulled alongside the curb where Rebecca waited with Les.

The back window slid down and Lilliana popped her head out. She waved to attract Rebecca's attention. "That boy inside took a big step tonight. Help him out. Agree to do the show."

Rebecca kissed Lilliana on the forehead. "I'm not so sure I can."

"Of course you can." Lilliana nodded in the direction of Rebecca's healing leg. "You never give up easy."

Rebecca refused Les's offer of a ride back to the city, knowing it would take him out of his way. Anyway, she had unfinished business to attend to.

Jake's crew had done a good cleanup job. Except for a few remaining coffee cups, the tables were clear. Bubbe had taken Jewel home earlier and all the guests were gone.

"Ready to call it a night, boss?" Vinnie dimmed the lights.

"I'll lock up. I've got one more thing to take care of."

"Ya gonna make sure that pretty little ballerina doesn't walk out of your life?"

"I'm going to give it my best shot." Jake loosened his bowtie and tossed his jacket over a chair.

"Don't let this one go. She's a keeper." Vinnie left through the back door.

Jake looked around the empty dining room. The affair had gone well, they survived the blackout, and even Morgan seemed to have mellowed. But for some reason the events seemed insignificant. Jake gathered the dirty cups and started in the direction of the kitchen when Rebecca walked back in."

"I just hailed a cab. The driver's willing to take me back to the city. He's already started the meter. I don't have much time." She spread her hands regretfully and waited for Jake to respond.

Jake placed the cups on a small tray. He thought of offering to drive her home. But if he did, he wouldn't want to leave her. Once he crossed the bridge onto her territory, the rules changed.

"I guess there's no time for our little talk." Leaning against the doorframe he watched her gather her belongings. "Have you given any thought to my offer?

"Do they expect me to wear a tutu?"

Jake wasn't sure if she was serious. He pictured her standing on the bridge in her bright red costume. He smiled. "Do you want to?"

"Of course I don't. It could be a fire hazard."

"Does that mean you'll do the show?" He didn't want to seem too eager.

"I'm not sure," she said, moving closer to him. "Is there room for negotiation?"

"More business talk. What do you have in mind?" Jake asked.

"No more business talk." Rebecca put her finger on his lip to silence him. Lilliana's words echoed. *You never give up.* "You're a complicated man. Very handsome, but very complex." She managed a serious frown. "Maybe it wasn't the passion of the event. Maybe I'm just another fool falling for a magnificent face."

"You won't be the first." Jake knew he deserved her bantering.

"Maybe it's not even you. I could be falling in love with your charming daughter or your delightful friends." She was being coy and playful.

He closed his hand around her fingers. "I think you've already won the hearts of my family and friends."

"That's important?" She had edged so close he was surprised the citrus scent of her shampoo still lingered in her hair.

"Very important." Although he resented their interference, his family and friends defined him.

"You're lucky to have them. Who else would protect you from all those single women out there?"

"Exactly." He looked down and saw the amusement in her face. It wasn't possible, but it felt like she had moved closer.

The dimly lit restaurant was silent. "We won't rush into anything." Rebecca's spoke in a whisper. "I'll do the cooking show if you'll join us July fourth in the Hamptons."

He didn't reply immediately. The TV show would be the prelude to the weekend in the Hamptons. "It's tempting. A weekend of fun and sun. No restaurant, fund raisers, or nosey relatives."

"What's your answer? The meter's running." Her voice was calm but insistent.

"You drive a hard bargain." Jake folded his arms and leaned back. He forgot he rested against the kitchen door. The door swung back.

Rebecca reached for him and they stumbled through the door together. Jake was quick and regained his footing on the other side. Rebecca rested against him. With his arms locked around her waist he realized she couldn't move if she wanted to.

He stared at her and then burst out laughing. "You really had me against the wall that time."

"I'm a woman on a mission." She tried to maintain a serious expression, but her lips twitched and she too broke into peals of laughter.

Their laughter was disturbed by a husky voice on the other side of the door. "Hey lady, you still want a cab?"

Chapter Twelve

While the makeup girl applied blush to her cheeks, Rebecca studied her reflection in the mirror. Her hair was secure in a tight bun. That was the easy part. Deciding what to wear had been more difficult. Rebecca had no idea what one wore to a cooking show. Something comfortable and safe but stylish. Did such an outfit exist? A simple blue linen shift had been her final choice.

"All those lights from the cameras can make you look pale." The girl's skilled hands highlighted Rebecca's high cheek bones. "Blue is a good color for you. You'll have the audience eating out of your hand."

Rebecca rubbed her hands together. Her palms were damp. During the cab ride from her uptown apartment to the downtown studio, all Rebecca could think about was how out of place she was going to feel behind a stove on national TV.

A young man stuck his head in the closet-sized room and announced, "We're ready to cook. Be on the set in five."

She and Jake had been kept in separate rooms. The producers explained they wanted the show to be spontaneous. It was going to be taped with a live audience. Her reactions to Jake's moves were expected to set the tone for the audience. She hoped it wouldn't turn into a comedy show.

Jake stood alone behind a long counter. He looked perfectly relaxed and within his element. Neatly arranged dishes were placed strategically in front of him. Rebecca recognized some of the more familiar ingredients like salt and pepper. She stood statue-like, waiting for her cue.

"Today we're going to prepare an elegant romantic brunch." Jake's large hands scrambled eggs in a ceramic bowl. With animated gestures he played to the TV audience. He greased a pan with butter, then added diced onions, mushrooms and fresh basil. Delicate puffs of steam flowed from the pan. Their aromas filled the studio. The crew watched with anticipation, anxious to taste the end result.

Rebecca looked on, hoping they would forget she was standing offstage. Jake was handling things fine on his own. No such luck.

"I could use some help here." Jake waved a whisk in the air, signaling for Rebecca to make her entrance. "For those of you who are not familiar with my assistant, meet Miss Rebecca Carr, prima ballerina with the City Ballet. When I first met this lovely lady, she didn't know salt from sugar."

Gentle applause came from the audience as Rebecca took her position beside Jake. "I wasn't that bad," she whispered to Jake.

"No secrets. Speak to the camera." A voice behind the set directed.

Rebecca knew there wasn't a script to direct them. For the most part, they were doing the show ad lib. She'd given impromptu performances before. She had danced for kings and queens with little preparation. For Rebecca, dancing was as easy as walking. But being expected to perform in the kitchen was like asking her to perform open-heart surgery.

"Do you know the one-handed technique for tossing?" Jake asked.

She was about to panic but Jake came to her rescue. Strong fingers locked over hers. He guided her as they chopped and tossed. With a little encouragement from him, she was soon dazzling her audience. He showed her how to toss and shake the pan full of vegetables. As they scrambled and sauteed they joked casually with each other. It couldn't have looked more natural if it had been rehearsed.

The brunch menu was completed with a mixed berry cake cooled with a scope of vanilla ice cream.

"Let's see if I can tempt my assistant with a taste."

The audience's applause encouraged Rebecca to sample the inviting dessert.

"Just a small taste." Rebecca never disappointed her fans. The flavor throbbed in her mouth as she swallowed the delectable dessert.

"It's a take." Someone behind the camera yelled. The cameras stopped rolling. The lights went on and the crew rushed forward to sample the feast.

"You were great." Jake placed a light kiss on Rebecca's forehead. Then he ushered her out of the way before they became part of the scrambled eggs.

As quickly as it started, the show was over. Once again

Rebecca had had an unexpected good time. For the past few days all she could think about was Jake. She had told herself that the attraction was purely physical, or that she was looking for an adventure to help pass the time until her troupe returned. There was so much more to Jake than his good looks. Even though he tried to convince her otherwise, she suspected he didn't want their escapade to end either.

"Excellent, excellent." The producer stepped forward with a plate in his hand. Between mouthfuls he said, "You two are a natural. The word from the booth is to offer you your own cooking show."

"That's great, Jake," Rebecca said.

"No, no. They want both of you," the producer added. "Little lady, you helped create one of the most elegant cooking shows I've ever seen."

"That's ridiculous." Rebecca was too startled by the suggestion to offer any sound objection.

"The chemistry between you is unbelievable." Cameramen and technicians began to gather around.

"The cook and the ballerina." Someone announced. "What a gimmick."

"We'll eat up the ratings. Excuse the pun." Everyone laughed.

"No, you don't understand." Rebecca finally found her voice. "I don't cook. I know nothing about food." Her eyes searched the crowd for Jake. "I don't even like to eat."

The more she objected, the more those around her agreed she was the perfect assistant.

"I'm sorry, I just don't have the time for another commitment." Rebecca stood firm.

"One evening a week is all we need to tape a series of shows." The producer found his way back to her side.

"I'm really not available, once the ballet season starts."

"What about you, Fleichman?"

"No deal." Jake stood against the wall. "We're a team. I can't do it without her." His thumbs hooked in the pockets of his jeans. He had a devilishly handsome grin on his face. The top buttons of his chef's tunic were undone, releasing the strain of the fabric against his broad shoulders.

She looked at Jake with surprise, realizing he found the whole incident amusing. "You're giving up easy."

"The lady's right. Use a little of that elusive magnetism to convince her. If I put out a call for a female assistant, there'd be a line from the studio door to Chinatown." The producer wasn't giving up.

"Her mind is made up. I doubt even my charm and good looks could convince her otherwise." Jake looked at Rebecca while he spoke to the producer. "What else do I have to bargain with? In return for her agreeing to do this show, I have to leave my restaurant on one of the most profitable weekends of the year."

"It's just food for thought. You don't have to give me an answer now," the producer said.

Rebecca watched the man walk away. She thought about what Jake had said. Her career was on hold while he still had a business to run. "Does it really put you in a bind leaving the restaurant July fourth?"

"I made a deal. You've held up your end. I can't go back on my word."

"I'm sure Dave would understand if you excused yourself," Rebecca said.

"Dave would understand." An arched brow indicated he found her remark humorous. "But would you?"

"I'd understand." Rebecca would never admit her disappointment if Jake didn't show up July fourth.

"Let's say we're even. No more deals or negotiations." Jake offered her his hand.

Rebecca nodded. If there was going to be something between them, their time together should be spontaneous, not some prearranged agreement.

"How are you getting out to the Hamptons?" Jake asked.

"The Hampton jitney." She began walking away.

Lilliana had expressed her concern about Rebecca's driving out alone. Weekend traffic on the Long Island Expressway was never faster than a crawl. Heading east on a holiday would be even worse. Lilliana suggested asking Jake or Les to drive out with Rebecca. Les already had plans. He was going out a day early to look at property in Montauk.

"Good idea. Let someone else hassle with the traffic," Jake said, slipping his arm around her as he caught up with her outside the dressing room.

"There might still be room on the bus," Rebecca said.

"Unfortunately I haven't decided when I'm leaving. All depends on how things go at the restaurant."

It took Rebecca about ten minutes to gather her belongings. When she reached the elevator Jake was already standing there. He held the door open. He had changed out of his chef's tunic into a Yankees T-shirt.

"I always took you for a Mets fan," Rebecca said.

"I am." Jake pressed the down button. "What about you? I remember you telling me you like baseball."

"Ever hear of Billy Carr?" Rebecca asked.

"Who hasn't. He pitches for one of the California teams."

"He's my brother." Rebecca stepped out of the elevator.

"Your brother?" Jake raised a brow. "I never made the association. How come you never mentioned him before?"

"The terms of our old agreement didn't allow us to share any personal information." She laughed.

"I'm glad we don't have to abide by those rules any longer. I'd like to know more about Rebecca Carr. You've been given a preview into my life. You've met my friends and family. Now it's my turn."

"Sounds fair to me." Rebecca placed her hand on his arm. "There's still a lot I don't know about Jake Fleichman." She felt his body tense. He wasn't ready to go there. She decided to change the subject. "How come you never think of me as part of the neighborhood?"

He turned to face her. "The people from the old neighborhood are solid, fixed in their positions." He brushed a stray wisp of hair off her face. "You're elusive, just like the fairy princesses in the stories I used to read to Jewel."

She had been compared to mysterious characters before— elves, nymphs, and pixies. But when Jake described her as an elusive princess, it did something to her that she couldn't explain. There was a sweetness in his answer that came from his heart.

Jake looked at his watch. "Do you have any plans for the rest of the evening?"

"What do you have in mind?"

"I know a nice little restaurant over the bridge. Very attentive staff. Good food. Excellent chef."

"Sounds good." Rebecca linked her arm in his and they headed for the garage where Jake had parked his car.

Rebecca was glad Jake phoned ahead. She didn't want to arrive at the restaurant and create a stir. She wanted the new phase of their relationship to get off to a good start.

"Dinner for two on the patio?" Vinnie asked when Jake and Rebecca entered.

Rebecca held her breath, remembering her last visit to

the secluded patio. It must be alluring now, the air fragrant from the scent of recently pinched herbs. The late afternoon sun would begin its descent, leaving a gentle shadow across the gray stone walk.

"It would be nice, but a private table in the dining room will be fine," Jake said. "I don't want to inconvenience the staff."

"Ya gonna sit there and act like a guest, or ya gonna snoop around the kitchen?"

"Is everything under control?" Jake asked.

"Under control." Vinnie reassured him.

"Okay then, we're in your hands."

The dinner procession began. First the wine steward appeared. He poured them each a glass of wine from a bottle in Jake's private collection.

"Good choice." Jake seemed pleased with the way things were going.

A line of busboys and waiters saw to their every need. Once they were satisfied that there was no more they could do, they disappeared.

To the unsuspecting diners seated nearby, they were just another young couple celebrating a special occasion.

For a brief moment there was an awkwardness between them of which they were both aware. Jake spread pumpernickel toast with garlic butter. Rebecca declined the portion he offered. She stroked her fork across her chicken.

"I'm sure my staff informed you the dish you're eating has been prepared in your honor."

Rebecca nodded. She sliced her chicken into tiny bite-sized pieces. Fork still in hand, she looked across the table. A playful smile curled her lips. "They also told me how you have developed a passion for oranges."

"Nothing is sacred with these guys."

"Your staff likes you a lot. They wouldn't take such liberties if they didn't."

"Fresh-squeezed orange juice on my desk every morning, orange slices on every entree I serve. They even ordered a mini orange tree from Florida."

Rebecca laughed. "Maybe I should change my scent."

"Never," Jake whispered. Before he could say any more there was a loud commotion from the direction of the kitchen. "What's going on?" Jake rushed to the door. "Wait here."

"Oh no," Rebecca said. She wasn't about to lose Jake in the depths of his kitchen. "I'm coming with you."

Jake placed his hand protectively around Rebecca's waist and led her into the kitchen. One of the assistant chefs was surrounded by the crew. A heavy frying pan hung by his side. His other hand held a dinner plate. Jake didn't rush in. Vinnie and the crew had calmed down the irate chef. He had become upset when a customer repeatedly insisted her tuna was undercooked.

"Tuna should never be killed by cooking." Vinnie pried the plate from the man's fingers. "But the customer must be satisfied."

Reluctantly the man released the plate. The fish had been seared beyond recognition.

"Sorry boss, I didn't mean to interrupt your dinner," the chef apologized to Jake and his co-workers.

"No harm done. Let's all just pick up where we left off." Jake and Rebecca returned to their meal. But someone on Jake's very efficient staff had cleared their table and was preparing to seat the next customer.

"We can have dessert in my office." Jake looked around the dining room. "Or on the patio."

Rebecca didn't want the evening to end, but she felt obligated to decline his offer. Jake had a situation to handle. He didn't need her standing in the wings waiting her turn for his attention. She followed his eyes around the crowded restaurant. "Is business always this good?"

"Every night."

"Hey boss, the tuna lady's still not pleased. She wants to speak to the chef. I think you better handle the situation before she makes a scene."

Jake reached for Rebecca's hand. "Why don't you have a seat at the bar."

They all looked in the direction of the already over-crowded bar.

Sitting alone at a crowded bar was not how Rebecca envisioned ending a near-perfect day. "I'd just be in the way." She saw the disappointed look on Jake's face and added. "I really had a good time. Thanks for insisting you couldn't do the show without me."

"Now all I have to do is hold up my end of the deal and make it out to the Hamptons."

Rebecca put her finger on his lip. "Remember no more negotiating. You'll give it your best shot. I'll understand if your other obligations get in the way."

"Are you giving up on me so soon?" Jake took both her hands in his. He kissed her open palm. "I can't think of anything that would keep me away."

Their casual chatter went back and forth for several minutes. Neither of them wanted the day to end. Standing off to the side, Vinnie cleared his throat.

"You've got work to do," Rebecca said.

"Tough choice. Go deal with the tuna lady or spend the rest of my evening with you." Before she could answer, he sighed. He took her hand and placed his lips on her inner wrist. Her pulse beat rapid beneath his kiss. "See you July fourth."

Rebecca entered the waiting taxi. She realized there was a good chance some strange mishap could prevent Jake from showing up in the Hamptons. She was never superstitious but she was beginning to believe the old wives' tale that things happened in threes. The blackout was number one, the tuna lady number two. She hoped she was wrong, but would an odd turn of events keep Jake away?

Chapter Thirteen

Exhausted by the slow crawl out to the Hamptons, Rebecca decided to rest before joining the party. Her accommodations exceeded her expectations. She would have been pleased to have a room in the Tudor-style mansion with a circular driveway as long as a high-school running track. However, she found herself in a beach house with an incredible view of the ocean. It didn't take long for images of asphalt and concrete to become distant memories, displaced by the tangy ocean breeze. It made the humid July day more than tolerable. After changing into a simple black bathing suit, she decided it was time to join the party.

Rebecca paused, then stepped through the French doors. She allowed the sights and smells of summer to assault her senses. Three-piece suits, high heels, and perfect coiffures were forgotten by the guests, who liberally poured suntan lotion on their already bronzed bodies.

The main celebration was planned for the next evening, but many guests had arrived early to avoid the holiday traffic. The deck around the pool was noisy and crowded. No one seemed to mind. The bright sky reflected off the inviting blue pool water. Rebecca decided to take a dip. The cool buoyancy welcomed her tired body. With gentle strokes she glided across the pool.

On the opposite end she hesitated a moment before surfacing. Her eyes stung from the heavy dose of chlorine. She shook her head rapidly to clear the water from her ears.

"Hi, Becky." There was a hint of a Brooklyn accent in the voice of the man who extended a helping hand.

Through her hazy gaze she couldn't mistake Les's tall, lanky form. She tried to hide her disappointment. "Hi, Les."

"Don't look so disenchanted." Les nodded in the direction of a cluster of lean muscular young men. "They couldn't wait for you to surface." Les handed her a towel. "Your boyfriend better get here soon, or he's going to have to compete with Dave's proteges."

"If you're referring to Jake, he's not my boyfriend."

"Whatever you say." Les shrugged. "Let's join our host."

Dave greeted Rebecca with a big bear hug. "Where's that boyfriend of yours?"

Les gave Rebecca an I-told-you-so look, before he excused himself and went off to join a group of bikini-clad young ladies.

"I'm sure Jake is sitting somewhere on the Long Island Expressway." She felt obligated to make an excuse for his absence.

"Don't worry, he'll show up." Dave offered her his arm. "I've got a group of overheated young men anxious to meet you."

The suntanned bodies that watched Rebecca swim across

the pool stood in unison as Dave and Rebecca approached. She wasn't sure if they stood in a mutual salute to Dave, or out of courtesy to her. Whatever the reason, they looked ready to pounce. Her fingers tightened around Dave's arm.

Dave patted her hand reassuringly. "Just smile and listen to them brag. They've got egos the size of Texas and checkbooks to match."

Rebecca seated herself facing the house. She wanted to make sure she spotted Jake as soon as he arrived. The hours passed, as Rebecca listened to the risks of buying stocks listed on the NASDAQ versus the big board.

The sun began to lower behind the house, and still no sign of Jake. Several of the young men escorted Rebecca back to the beachhouse so that she could change for dinner. She changed into a linen sundress and rejoined her new friends for a casual poolside dinner. They were joined by Les and an attractive stockbroker. Having exhausted all their tales earlier, the conversation centered around the cost of living in the city.

When Rebecca decided to call it a night, one over-attentive young man insisted on walking her back to the beach house. "You sure you'll be okay all alone there?"

With only a few scattered lights along the walk, it was impossible to see. The sound of the surf and smell of the sea air told her they weren't far from the blue and white shingled beach house.

She stopped short and turned to face her escort. "Thank you." She offered her hand.

"You going into that empty house all alone?" The young man closed both his hands over hers.

"I don't mind." She slipped her hand free and reached for the door knob. She had a hard time convincing him it wasn't necessary to accompany her inside. The one man she was interested in had let her down. It was all Jake's fault she was in this situation now. She suddenly felt very upset with Jake Fleichman. Her abrupt change in temperament must have been reflected in her tone. "See you tomorrow."

The young man finally got the message. "Tomorrow will be fine." He didn't look back.

She leaned against the door and breathed a sigh of relief. The huge porch that stretched along the rear of the house looked inviting. She stepped outside. Gray clouds hid the light of the moon.

Even as a small child, Rebecca never had a fear of the dark. It provided solitude. A time to be alone. The chance to probe her thoughts. Her eyes began to adjust to the dark. Sand dunes lined the path beyond the house. She closed her eyes so that her mind could focus.

She highlighted the events that brought her to this evening. Jake's slow turnaround. His sudden awakening to his feelings. The surge of passion she felt when they kissed.

Completely lost in an illusion of privacy, she didn't move when her hair slipped from its restraining clip. The ocean wind tossed her ends gently across her shoulders. Someone had released the clasp. The unexpected distraction startled her at first. Who had dared to interrupt her privacy? The first person who came to mind was the stockbroker who had walked her home. What nerve, she thought. She raised her elbow and smashed it into the intruder's ribs at the same time her heel crushed hard against his foot.

"Blast it, Rebecca."

Rebecca let out a gasp when she recognized the strong, husky voice. She turned, as Jake collided with the lounge chair in his haste to escape her wrath. He sat at the end of the seat. One hand guarded his rib cage, the other raised in a peace offering.

"What are you doing here?" Rebecca rubbed the sore spot on her elbow. "Your chest is like a brick wall."

"And your punch is like a wrecking ball. You've got a lot of wallop, for a little lady who doesn't eat much."

"I'm sorry, but I didn't expect you. I thought I was alone." She sat down next to him.

A small red blotch began to form over his left ribs. Rebecca reached up to massage the area. Jake grabbed her hand just as her fingertips grazed his skin.

"Does it hurt?" Her fingers rested gently on his chest.

"Not that much." Jake splinted his ribs with his hand. He walked over to the deck rail. "I'll be fine."

Rebecca studied his shirtless back. She assumed he'd be in good shape, with the well-equipped gym he had. However, she hadn't expected to see such toned muscle definition. "What are you doing here?"

"I was invited. Sorry I'm late."

Little drops of water glistened on his skin. His hair appeared recently tousled by towel-drying. He looked as if he had just stepped out of the shower. Her shower.

She jumped up. The realization hit her full force. "You're staying here too. In this house."

"It would seem that way." His smile told her he approved of the arrangements.

"Do you think there was a mistake?"

"Not at all." Jake said. "I think our fairy godparents, Lilliana and Dave, have arranged for us to share this great beach house."

"It is nice, isn't it?" The combination of beach and ocean softened her mood. She stretched her arms over her head and inhaled deeply. The wet salt air filled her nostrils. "It's even nicer in daylight."

Jake stepped closer. "I think the view is fine right now."

"You don't mind their meddling?"

"Not at all. Lilliana's concern is for your happiness. She wants whatever's right for you. She and I have the same interest."

"Oh really?"

"Yes, we both know what you need."

"And what is it I need?"

"More precisely it's who you need." Jake put his arms around her waist. He drew her close. "A perfect fit."

Rebecca tilted her head up. He looked into eyes as dark as the starless night. Crushing her to him, he pressed his mouth to hers. The moist air set her hair in tight ringlets around her face and down her back. He grasped her curls in his fist as if he feared their silky softness would slip away. She slipped her arm around him. Her touch was soft but it brushed across his bruise.

"Ouch."

"Still hurts?"

"Just a little sore."

"Wait here, I'll get some ice."

Rebecca caught her reflection in the window. She decided to freshen her lipstick before returning to the porch. When she returned, Jake was stretched out on the lounge chair fast asleep.

The morning sun inched its way above the horizon.

Sleeping on a lounge chair was not how Jake envisioned spending his first evening in the Hamptons. What he needed was a jog on the beach followed by a swim. Only one problem, his clothes were behind the closed door. Jake hesitated. His hand rested on the brass knob. What if she was already awake. He listened. There was dead silence behind the door. He couldn't stand there forever, especially if he wanted to be away when she woke up.

Heavy drapes shut tight kept out the morning sun. Once his eyes adjusted to the dark, Jake could make out the small form. She lay curled into a tight ball at the edge of the kingsize bed. Only one well-shaped leg escaped the confines of its cover. It amazed him how lifeless she slept. He grabbed his clothes, running shoes, and a towel. A long vigorous workout was what he needed. If it didn't kill him, maybe it would at least give him time to think.

Today was the fourth. The day of the big celebration. Breakfast was being served poolside. It would be served all morning, lead into lunch, and end with a big bang after dinner. Rebecca didn't feel like celebrating. She slipped into shorts and a T-shirt. She was surprised to find Jake had already left the beach house.

Trays of fresh fruits surrounded the crepe chef. Dave and Lilliana were seated at a table with several guests. Two bikini-clad women sat on either side of Les. One of the women looked like an overstuffed pumpkin in her shocking orange swimsuit. The other looked like she should borrow some flesh from her friend.

"Mind if I join you?" Rebecca asked.

"We've been waiting for you." Les shifted his chair over, to make room beside him.

"I saw Jake on the beach early this morning." Lilliana looked over her stack of apple-filled crepes. "He jogged." She put a forkful into her mouth. "Then he swam." She wiped the syrup off her lip. "One more event and he would have his own personal triathalon."

"I don't know how anyone can have so much energy so early in the day." Les stifled a yawn.

Rebecca paid little attention to their idle chatter. Her eyes searched the clusters of guests.

"Look at that one." Miss Pumpkin pushed her sunglasses to the tip of her nose. "Ah, he's coming this way."

Everyone turned to see who she was talking about.

Rebecca felt her heart beat in her throat. Jake approached. His bare chest did not seem out of place among the other scantly clad diners. His body glistened with sweat.

"Good morning." He reached for a glass of freshly squeezed juice from a passing waiter. "Nice day?" His smile reached everyone seated around the table. He came around the table to where Rebecca sat. Resting his hands on her shoulders he massaged gently. "Did you sleep well?"

Dave and Lilliana exchanged knowing glances. Rebecca wanted to tell them that nothing had come out of their little scheme.

A waiter brought a chair for Jake. He positioned it next to Dave. The bikini women commented on Rebecca's control at the buffet table. They started questioning her about her life as a dancer.

Rebecca was more interested in hearing what Jake had to say to Dave. They spoke in hushed tones. Dave scribbled some notes on a napkin.

"Consider it done," Dave said.

"I knew I could count on you." Jake shook Dave's hand and acknowledged Rebecca with a nod. "See you later."

Her fairy godparents didn't give Rebecca time to show her disappointment in Jake's sudden departure. They hustled her off to meet their guests. One or the other kept her occupied until late afternoon, when she finally begged off for a break.

When Rebecca opened the door of the beach house, she was overtaken by a powerful fragrance: the scent of roses. Airy clusters of Queen Anne's lace and deep green leaves provided a sharp contrast for vases filled with the palest peach porcelena roses. Elegant long-stemmed red roses, petite rose bushes in mint green ceramic pots, and silvered lavender roses in trumpet-shaped vases filled every empty space in the room. Stunned by the unexpected display, she stood still for a moment before starting a mad search for a note, an explanation.

Her answer came in the most unexpected way. A little man in a black suit, one of Dave's house staff, emerged from the patio. "Mr. Fleichman requests your presence at a private dinner party. Be ready in an hour." Then the man vanished.

The whole thing was so absurd Rebecca found herself laughing out loud. The stage had been set for an enchanted evening. Jake Fleichman had surprised her again. Only this time it was the most pleasant of surprises. Nothing could happen to change her mood. She stood in the room full of roses and laughed until her sides ached. Then she rushed off to change for her magical evening.

In precisely one hour the man in black reappeared. She followed him away from the house through the dunes.

In bare feet Jake waited by the surf. He had rolled his pants legs above his ankles and wore a shirt opened at the neck. A white tablecloth was spread across the sand. Champagne glasses, dinner, and roses rested on it. Music from the house played beach tunes.

"Can you shag?" Jake asked.

"I don't think I ever have."

"This is a night for firsts." He offered her his hands, palms up. Lightly her fingers rested against his skin. He turned her hands over and brushed his lips over her palms. Then he kissed each finger separately. It felt as if an electric shock passed through her.

"Come dance with me." Jake began to sway to the soft music. "I don't like to dance alone."

"I don't think I can do this."

"Sure you can." Jake opened his arms for her. "You're a dancer, aren't you?"

Rebecca accepted his invitation. His hand found the small of her back and drew her closer. She accepted his unspoken invitation to lean against him.

"Just follow me."

Following her partner came naturally to Rebecca. Surprisingly Jake moved with perfect rhythm as they glided over their sandy dance floor.

"Where did you learn to do this?"

"In another life, I worked as a sous chef in North Carolina." He had stopped dancing but held her close. "It was a long time ago."

"Want to tell me about it?"

"How long do you have?"

"A lifetime, if needed."

They sat down on the sand. "It was the summer I met Johanna."

"Jewel's mother?"

Jake nodded. "I guess ocean breezes have a strange effect on me."

"I hope this isn't a passing fancy." Rebecca tried to make light of the conversation.

He took her hands. "You were always right under my nose. In a little red schoolhouse on Ocean Parkway." Releasing her hands he waved his in the direction of the sea. "All this is a bonus."

"Les told me Johanna was a chef too."

Jake laughed. "That's Morgan for you. Can't even let me tell my own story. It was a match made in the kitchen. It all seemed so perfect. She wanted international fame. We accepted positions in Brazil, some big fancy hotel."

"How long did you live in South America?"

"Awhile. Then we moved to Toronto."

"You've lived everywhere."

"Seems like that, but I always come back to Brooklyn."

"Was Johanna happy to move back?"

"For awhile. We opened the Bridge Cafe and were an overnight success." Jake picked up some broken shells and pitched them into the surf. "When Jewel was born, Johanna felt tied down. I suppose she felt she'd never have the fame and fortune she wanted."

"If she had waited, it would have come." Rebecca released a heavy sigh. "You're so successful now."

"Johanna was too impatient. Some hotel tycoon came along and offered her an opportunity on a grander scale. One that gave her international fame and a jetset lifestyle." Jake laughed with a sharp, cynical chuckle. "We did agree on one thing—that was not the life we wanted for Jewel."

"So you stayed behind to raise your daughter," Rebecca said. "And Johanna?"

"She feel in love with the lifestyle that he gave her, and eventually she fell in love with him."

"Foolish woman," Rebecca whispered.

With both hands Jake turned her face toward his. His lips brushed across her forehead. "I haven't told this story in a long time. But I'm glad I told you. Anything else you want to know?"

"Want to tell me about your constant bickering with Les?"

"That's been going on since high school. I was the jock with all the friends. He was the rich kid with all the money. I wanted to be him and he wanted to be me."

Jake's story ended just as the first fireworks tinted the sky. For a short time they put away their memories and allowed themselves to be lost in the childish excitement of the July Fourth celebration. They held hands, anticipating the next flash of light and color. When the last burst of sparkles and twinkles faded away, Jake helped Rebecca to her feet.

"We never finished our dance," he said.

"There's no music."

"Listen." Jake leaned toward the shore.

Rebecca strained to hear even a hint of a melody. Jake pulled her close, so close she felt every breath he took. They swayed to the sound of the surf and their heartbeats.

"Excuse me, Sir." The little man in black cleared his throat. "There's an important call for you at the house."

A flicker of apprehension crossed Jake's face. "Bubbe is the only one who knows this number."

"It's probably nothing." She tried to reassure him.

"Wait here." He kissed her on the cheek. "I'll be right back."

"Haven't got any place better to go." It was a poor attempt at making light of a possibly grave situation. Rebecca could have wished him a happy Fourth of July or a Merry Christmas. It didn't matter what she said. He didn't hear a word. He was already racing toward the main house.

Rebecca walked closer to the ocean. She played tag with the surf, daring the waves to wash across her feet. The cool water felt good. She couldn't remember a time when her feet didn't ache. She stared down at her toes. So knotted and bent from years of defying gravity. Dancing had taken its toll on her body. Perhaps it was time for her to seriously adjust her career. So many ex-dancers redirected into another related career. She could teach. There would always be a full-time position for her at the ballet academy. Maybe just one more season. She buried her feet in the sand and waited for Jake to return.

Jake prided himself in his athletic abilities, but his feet had never felt this heavy as he ran in the sand. The little man in the black suit had a hard time following. It looked as if the poor man had just run a marathon and come in dead last. Aside from the fright on his face, Jake hardly showed any signs of strain.

"In here." The man pointed to a side entrance.

Fortunately none of the other guests were around. No one delayed Jake as he made a mad dash for the antique table where the phone rested. It could have been sitting on a piece of driftwood, the way Jake reached for it.

Rebecca returned to the blanket. She stared mindlessly at the remaining sulfuric clouds as they drifted across the smoke-filled sky.

"All alone on such a pretty night?"

The unexpected voice startled her. "Les, what are you doing out here?"

"I was taking a little walk on the beach. I saw someone who looked a lot like Fleichman running to the house. I thought I'd investigate."

"Jake had a phone call." She tried to sound calm.

"Must be serious if he left all this." Les raised a bushy brow as he scanned the empty wine glasses and fancy dinner setup. "One of his sous chefs could have forgotten a recipe."

"Be serious. I have a feeling it doesn't have anything to

do with the restaurant." Rebecca hugged her knees to her chest.

It seemed like an eternity before Jake returned. He came around the side of the dune, unknown to either Rebecca or Les.

"Jake," Rebecca gasped.

"Sorry, I didn't mean to scare you." There were tense lines across his brow. "Morgan, I'm glad you're here. I've got to leave tonight. Would you mind driving Rebecca back to the city Monday?"

Les was speechless when Jake said he was glad to see him. He nodded in agreement.

"Thanks, I've got to leave tonight," Jake repeated, with an anxious cough.

Rebecca had never seen Jake so apprehensive. Always calm and in control of every situation, he seemed to be trying very hard to hold his emotions in check.

"What is it? What happened? Who called?"

"It's Jewel. Some stomach thing."

"I'm sure it's nothing," Morgan said. "You know how kids are. Probably one hot dog too many at a barbecue."

Rebecca ignored Morgan. What did he know about children? But then, who was she to talk. What did she know about children? Jake was the little girl's father, while both she and Les were outsiders with no experience in raising a child.

"Is it serious?" As soon as the words were out, Rebecca realized what a dumb question she asked. It must be serious if his family was willing to disrupt his mini-vacation. They had been so adamant that he leave everything in their capable hands.

"I don't know. They called from the emergency room."

"Where? What hospital?"

"My mother and Vinnie took her to Maimonides. The doctors are waiting for the test results." Jake turned to leave. "I should be there if they have to admit her."

"Maybe you should drive back with him." Les nudged her in Jake's direction. "I'll explain to Dave and Lilliana."

"You'd do that for Jake?"

"No, I'm doing it for you. It's what you really want to do. Isn't it?"

"Thanks. Tell Lilliana I'll call her when we get to Brooklyn." She ran to keep up with Jake's long strides. "Wait for me."

Jake stopped. They almost collided. He put his hands on her shoulders to prevent them both from falling.

"I'd like to drive back with you. How can I enjoy the rest of the weekend, knowing you're sitting in the hospital with your daughter?"

"I can't ask that of you." Jake's brow was still knotted with worry. "It's not your responsibility. One of us should enjoy the remainder of the weekend."

"You're not asking. I'm offering," Rebecca said.

"I know Jewel would like to see you."

"It's settled, I'm coming with you." Rebecca studied his face. "If you want me to?"

Pulling her to him, he pressed his mouth to hers. Rebecca had the answer she needed. They packed in a hurry. Rebecca picked up a random sock. She stuffed it into the pocket of a pair of shorts and tossed it on top of the pile of clothes in her blue suitcase. Jake was even more haphazard. The sleeve of a T-shirt hung out the side of his suitcase.

"I'll get the car while you explain to our hosts." Jake was already out the door.

Rebecca decided to leave through the big house. It

wasn't that she didn't trust Les, but it seemed rude if she didn't explain in person to Dave.

Les stood in a corner with Lilliana. The horrified look on Lilliana's face told Rebecca that he had explained the situation. Rebecca went in search of their host. Buffet tables lined the walls of the dining room. Dave was nowhere to be seen.

The pungent scent of hickory floated through the open French doors. Rebecca stepped out onto the patio. She spotted Dave immediately. Dressed in an apron and oven mitts, he tossed and turned ribs, burgers, and hot dogs over red-hot coals. Rebecca inched her way through the hungry crowd. As soon as Dave saw her, he gestured for her to join him.

"Some of the local celebrities are here tonight. I think you should meet them." Dave passed his spatula on to the attentive cook guarding the grill.

Rebecca knew Jake was anxious to start back to the city. Every attempt to pull Dave off to the side was foiled by another introduction to a local movie star or famous personality. Some were fans of Rebecca's, interested in Lilliana's school. She couldn't just brush them off. It only took a minute to smile and thank them. But the minutes added up, as she was escorted from one well-wisher to another. Dave was no longer at her side when she glanced at her watch and realized that a precious half-hour had passed.

Jake pulled the car around the circular driveway and waited for Rebecca. He dared not go inside to find her, for fear of getting caught up in the festivities.

A young valet approached. "Can I help you, Sir?"

Jake turned his wrist for a glimpse at his watch. "Yes, please take the blue suitcase out and see that it's brought to the beach house."

Jake knew a lot of people involved in the arts had been invited to join the party. Maybe Rebecca met some old friends and had decided to stay. As a single parent, his choices were different. He doubted she could imagine the turmoil his mind was in. His little girl alone in a hospital. In pain. Strangers probing her, drawing blood, poking her with needles. He had already waited too long. He turned the key in the ignition and headed west.

Finally free from the endless introductions, Rebecca decided Lilliana would have to explain the situation to Dave. Rebecca slipped out a side door and made her way to the front of the house. In a hurry to join Jake, she had a near collision with a young man carrying a suitcase. Immediately she recognized it.

"Where are you taking that?"

"To the beach house."

"There must be some mistake. That's mine. I'm leaving this evening."

"Are you Miss Carr?"

"Yes."

"Mr. Fleichman said to give you this note." The boy waited.

Slowly, half in anticipation, half in alarm, Rebecca unfolded the note.

> *Have a nice weekend.*
> *Call me when you get back.*
> *Jake*

Rebecca crumpled the paper in her hand. She stared down at her clenched fist. That was it. A note. See you later.

The boy cleared his throat, reminding her she was not alone. "Should I take this to the beach house?"

"Yes, thank you." She started to follow the young man but decided she didn't want to return to the empty house. She didn't feel like rejoining the party either. The festive mood had evaded her.

Perhaps the beach would soothe her. She walked along the shore. A mild breeze blew the hem of her dress. She concentrated on the sound of the waves breaking. The surf, the salt air, and the movement of the sea helped clear her senses. She could think rationally now. He hadn't abandoned her; she was the one who left him alone when he needed her.

She found herself in front of the dunes where they had dined and danced. How everything had changed in only a few short hours. Nothing remained—the tablecloth, food, and wine had disappeared as mysteriously as they had appeared.

Rebecca glided her left foot along the damp sand. Her arms reached out to her sides. She hugged her arms around her waist, but they were no substitute for Jake's strong hands guiding her to the rhythm of the surf.

She had no idea how long she was out there. The lights from the big house were dim. Only a waning moon lit the sky. The air had turned cooler. A sudden chill made her shiver. She had the feeling someone was watching her.

"You can't be cold." Jake stood behind her, his hands on her shoulders.

"Jake?" Rebecca did not turn around. She feared her mind was playing tricks. "What are you doing here? What about Jewel?"

His fingers massaged deep into her muscles, assuring her

he was really there. He stopped for a moment. "I called the hospital from the car."

"But . . ." Rebecca turned to face him. He put his finger on her lips to silence her.

He looked so good, his silhouette highlighted by the dimmed lights from the house. Maybe he wasn't real. She could have conjured him here. He stood almost face to face with her.

She watched his lips move, heard the words, "It's a long drive back to Brooklyn. I called the hospital from the car. Jewel's fine."

She heard herself respond, "She's in the hospital? She's admitted?"

"The doctor ruled out appendicitis. They're sending her home."

"Then you don't have to go back." The twinge of guilt she felt slipped away.

"We'll go back in the morning." Jake stifled a yawn. "Right now, there's a lounge chair calling my name."

Chapter Fourteen

T he ride back to Brooklyn was uneventful. Rebecca offered to drive part of the way. Jake refused, so she sat back
and relaxed. They hardly spoke. A bouquet of mixed-color
roses lay across the back set. Their fragrance filled the car,
reminding Rebecca of the magic of the weekend.

They arrived at Jake's house just as Bubbe and Jewel
were sitting down to breakfast.

"Look who's here. It's Dad and Miss Becky," Jewel announced with the energy of child who had never been ill a
day in her life.

"Don't you look fine." Jake scooped her up in his arms.

"I feel great. Hi, Miss Becky." Jewel's eyes twinkled
when she smiled. "I've got an idea. Why don't we all go
have pancakes at Mort's, then we can take Miss Becky
across the bridge."

174

Bubbe intervened. "You, young lady, are going to have some toast and tea. We've got to get you well, so you can get on the bus to summer camp in three days."

"That's exactly why we have to go today." Jewel placed her hands on her hips and stood her ground. "I'll be away all summer. Who's going to see that Miss Becky gets to walk across the Brooklyn Bridge?"

"I think maybe your father and Miss Becky are tired from their long drive. Go eat." Bubbe gave Jewel a gentle pat on her rear. She gestured for her grandson and his guest to join them. "Sit. I'll make you coffee."

Jewel expounded on her treatment in the emergency room. Even thought the doctor and nurses were extremely nice and apologized every time they had to stick her with a needle, she was never going back there again. When everyone agreed with her that it must have been an unpleasant experience, she dropped the subject.

"I wouldn't mind if you and Dad did the bridge without me." Jewel was so insistent that they promised to go next weekend, and send her letters about their day.

Bubbe instructed Jewel to help clear the table, allowing Jake and Rebecca a few minutes alone. Jake guided her out onto the little balcony overlooking the promenade. Below them sanitation crews were busy removing the liter from the previous evening's celebration.

"Sometime this week I'd like to have a little dinner party for everyone." Jake leaned against the rail. He looked tired.

"Sounds like a great idea, but right now I think you need to rest." Rebecca checked her watch. "You aren't going to run off to the restaurant as soon as I leave?"

"You know me pretty well, don't you." Jake put his hand on her arm. "And you're going to do a little workout."

"Touché." Rebecca slipped from his grasp.

"Don't forget about next weekend," Jake said as she walked away.

"Next weekend?" She turned before going into the house.

"You forgot already?" On the river below a foghorn echoed a disappointed bellow. "I'll have a very unhappy daughter if she doesn't get mail from us describing our walk."

"Can we skip Mort's?" Rebecca asked.

"I don't think so. She's a stickler for details."

"Just like her father," Rebecca said. "Don't worry, I'll be there."

Traffic in the city was light until the taxi reached Columbus Circle. Her driver wove around the other yellow cabs searching for early fares. Rebecca told him to let her out in front of Lincoln Center. She paid the fare and walked the short distance to her apartment building.

Before Rebecca went upstairs she stopped at the concierge desk. An oversized envelope was waiting. She read the return address. It was from somewhere in France. She decided it must be from one of her colleagues and tucked it into her bag.

Wrapped in a soft robe, her wet hair twisted in a towel, Rebecca stepped from the steamy bathroom. She poured a diet soda and gathered her mail. With her legs curled under her she opened the thick envelope from France. Inside was an airplane ticket to London, a program, and a short note.

Tried to call you. No answer. Sent the ticket anyway. Scheduled to do a command performance for the Queen. Prima ballerina injured. You're the only one

*who can take her place on short notice. Be prepared
to join us for remainder of tour.*

Jacques

Rebecca studied the program. The performance was
scheduled for next weekend. She reached for the phone,
anxious to share the good news with Jake. Here was her
chance to show Jake her world. She'd invite him to join
her. They could send Jewel a card from London Bridge
instead of Brooklyn Bridge. She hesitated. It would be better to ask Jake in person. She wanted to see the reaction
on his face.

Fortunately, Dave and Lilliana arrived back in the city
early. Jake had invited everyone to The Bridge on Tuesday
night. The restaurant was crowded, as usual.

As soon as Rebecca arrived, Vinnie grabbed her by the
arm and escorted her out to the patio. "Jake's arranged an
intimate dinner for six."

Lilliana, Dave, Les, and Bubbe were already seated. The
men stood up as Rebecca approached. She didn't realize
Jake was directly behind her. He held out her chair. Once
she was seated, he took the seat next to her's.

"To a job well done." Jake raised his glass in a toast to
the group."

"The school will be better than ever," Lilliana said. To
everyone's surprise, she touched her glass to the one Les
held. "Even this gonif has helped."

Les acknowledged the older woman with a nod. "I have
agreed to put all the monies raised into the capable hands
of Dave's accountants."

Again everyone raised their glasses, this time to toast
Dave Burke. The salutes continued throughout the dinner.

She overheard Dave telling Jake how much he liked to dance now, and how he can't wait to take Lilliana in his arms and twirl her round the room. The other day his secretary had caught him doing a soft-shoe in his office.

Rebecca found it amusing when she tried to picture the man who would cut your throat from market opening to closing bell gracefully gliding Lilliana around a room. Rebecca's feet shuffled under the table as she remembered dancing with Jake on the beach. She had had many partners, world renowned dancers, but none made her feel like she did in Jake's arms. Jake had a similarly dreamy look in his eyes. Was he remembering dancing to the beach music too?

Somehow Jake managed to spend the entire evening with his guests. Rebecca wondered if she should announce her news in front of the entire group. She never got the chance.

Dave had an announcement of his own. He reached for Lilliana's hand and helped her to her feet. "Should you tell them, or should I?" He looked at Lilliana.

"Dave has asked me to marry him." Lilliana spoke just above a whisper.

"Mazel tov." Bubbe was the first to offer her good wishes.

"Congratulations." Everyone echoed her sentiment.

Rebecca tried to hide the play of emotions on her face. Of course she was happy. She adored both Lilliana and Dave. She rushed around the table and gave them both a huge hug.

She heard Jake's voice. "I'm thrilled for both of you. Have you decided on a date?"

"We're not kids like you two. The sooner the better."

"Where do you plan to have the wedding?" Jake asked.

"If we hold the ceremony and reception at my home in

the Hamptons, we can invite the entire financial and dance world."

Rebecca turned to Jake, her nose wrinkled in objection to Dave's plan. Jake interrupted before Dave could elaborate. "I don't think Rebecca likes the idea."

"What is it you don't like, little lady?"

"It's not for me to say." She looked at her dance teacher. "Has he asked you how you feel about a big celebration?"

Rebecca accepted Lilliana's silence as a no. "Lilliana is a private person. One of the reasons she never moved her school into Manhattan was to avoid extra attention."

"Is that really what you want?" he asked Lilliana.

"Becky knows me well. I'd like to keep it simple." Lilliana squeezed Dave's hand.

"I didn't realize. Whatever you want. We'll limit it to a few close friends," Dave said.

"If you really want to keep this quiet, I have a suggestion." Jake's lips curled in a convincing smile.

"Please continue." Dave gestured for Jake to speak. "I value your opinion too."

"It would be my pleasure to create a simple but elegant affair at The Bridge."

"And Manny will make such a beautiful cake," Bubbe announced.

Dave raised his hand palms up, signaling for everyone to stop. "Absolutely not. You're coming as a guest. We have some excellent caterers on Long Island." Dave sat erect and threw out his chest. "A man in my position knows how to have things done his way."

"I have to confess my reasons are selfish. I want to do it as a wedding present. What could I possibly give to a man in your position?" Jake imitated Dave's pompous stance.

"I've known Lil my whole life. I should let a stranger make her wedding cake?" Bubbe said.

Dave laughed and turned toward Rebecca. "See what you've started."

Rebecca hesitated, torn by conflicting emotions. If Jake involved himself with the same enthusiasm he had for the last event, he would have no time for a trip to London. "How soon are you planning to do this?" she asked.

"This week, next week, whenever Lilliana says go," Dave said.

Rebecca envied the love in Dave's voice. She heard the enchantment every time he whispered Lilliana's name. She watched Jake take a sip of his cognac. Did he say her name in hushed tones when she left the room?

Lilliana didn't want Jake to rush into planning an affair so soon after the fund raiser. She also wanted Jewel to be her flower girl. Before the evening ended, they agreed on a date in September.

Rebecca was left alone on the patio with Jake. He placed some empty glasses on a tray and started toward the restaurant.

"I'm not letting you leave just yet." Rebecca planted her feet firmly on the ground blocking his path. "I've got something to show you." She reached into her large bag and pulled out the envelope with the airplane tickets.

Jake put down the tray and pulled out a chair.

Rebecca chose the chair on the other side of the table. She wanted to study his face as he read the destination.

"This must be important, you look so serious." Jake reached for the envelope.

Mockingly he picked it up with caution. He studied all four corners. He held it up to his nose. He tossed it hand-to-hand as if it burnt his palms.

"Will you stop acting like it's going to blow up." She raised her chin in a dignified position.

"And the winner is." Jake gave her a slanted look. "There *is* a winner in here?"

"I think so." Rebecca couldn't contain her enthusiasm. She walked around the table, grabbed the envelope, pulled out its contents, and scattered an assortment of papers across the table. "Here, it's two tickets to London." She sat down next to him and waited for his response.

He raised a brow. "London?" There was caution in his voice. "Two tickets? For who?"

"You and me." She had thought it was such a good idea to invite him and surprise him with a ticket.

"We're going to Europe?" Jake combed his fingers through his hair. "You bought me a ticket?"

"Yes we leave Thursday." She hesitated, not sure she had made the right decision. "I'm going to dance the Firebird for the Queen."

"How long will you be gone?"

"They want me to stay with the troupe until the tour is over."

"You can't expect me to follow you from one city to the next." Jake shifted the ticket from one hand to the other, as if it weighed more than he could handle.

"No, just London. I understand you have obligations." Determined to convince him how wonderful a trip to London would be, she babbled on. "You can see me perform and if you don't fly right back, we can tour the city. Just think how thrilled Jewel will be when she gets our cards from England."

"I'd love to see you dance. You must be excited to give a royal performance." He reached out and caught her hand in his. "It all sounds so great. But I can't go. I can't just pick up and leave on command. Even if it is a royal command. I followed someone once before. It didn't work out."

"I'm not asking you to give up your life and follow me. I'm inviting you to join me in London." She gave a choked, desperate laugh. "For a weekend."

"It sounds like it's important to you. You go. I'll be here when you get back."

"The royal performance means nothing to me. I'd rather know you were watching. I've spent my summer falling in love with your world. Isn't it time I introduced you to mine?" She was glad he didn't notice the tremor in her voice.

"I'm sorry, Becky. I can't go." The tone of his voice was infinitely compassionate.

"How will you explain to Jewel that we didn't follow her instructions?"

"She'll get over it. We'll do Mort's and the bridge when you get back. Things come up. I understand." He said the last words with the certainty of a man who had said them before.

Rebecca gathered her tickets and tossed them into her satchel. She didn't hear him tenderly whisper her name.

For the next two days Rebecca drowned herself in practice. She called an old dance partner she knew was in the city for the summer, and asked him to dance the role of the prince. He helped her practice, but she didn't need it. Rebecca knew the part of the Firebird too well.

One day after rehearsal he asked her, "What's wrong Becky? You usually glow with satisfaction after you dance this part."

She did something she hadn't done in a long time: she

shared her feelings with someone else. "There's someone I really wanted to join me in London."

"If you don't want to go, maybe you shouldn't." He offered her some orange slices.

Rebecca smiled as she removed the fruit from the peel. "I wish the Firebird's magic could give me the answer."

"Nobody can tell you what to do. You have to follow your heart."

"You're right, but it's been a long time since I've followed my heart." Rebecca kissed her partner on the forehead. "Thanks for the help."

The next morning Rebecca was up before the sun. Around ten A.M. she buzzed her doorman and requested a taxi. As she stepped out onto the street, a yellow cab pulled up to the curb.

"Where to, lady?" the cab driver asked.

"Kennedy Airport, please." Rebecca tossed her satchel onto the seat beside her.

At the British Airways terminal she stepped from the cab and rushed inside. Last night her plan had seemed so sound. She even imagined Jake meeting her at the airport. As she approached the security gate, someone called her name.

A young woman with her hair wrapped in a tight bun rushed forward. She threw her arms around Rebecca's neck. "Thank you, thank you. I can't believe you're giving up this performance. This chef must be something special."

"He is." Rebecca pressed the airplane ticket into the girl's hand. "I'll tell you all about him when you get back."

The girl thanked Rebecca one more time, before she disappeared in the crowd of travelers.

Rebecca's decision had been made. There was no turning back. Before leaving the terminal, she had a call to make.

"Bridge Cafe," the voice on the other end said.

"Jake Fleichman please," Rebecca said.

"Sorry, the boss is out. Went for a walk."

"Can I speak to Vinnie?"

"He's out too. Went to the market for the boss."

Rebecca hung up. It was odd for Jake to be away from the restaurant if he hadn't gone to the market. She searched through her bag for more loose change. She had to call Bubbe. If anyone knew where Jake was, his grandmother would.

"The boy hasn't been himself since the dinner party. Wants to be alone." Bubbe sighed on the other end of the phone. "He takes long walks from one end of the Brooklyn Bridge to the other. You'd think he lost something."

"He's taking walks over the bridge." Rebecca repeated Bubbe's words.

"Unless he's related to the man upstairs, he's not walking on the water."

"Thanks, Bubbe." Rebecca knew where she would find Jake. She ran out of the terminal and stepped into the first taxi she saw.

"You again," the driver said. "That was a short trip."

"I decided not to go." Just what she needed, a cabby who remembered his last fare. "Can you take me to the Manhattan side of the Brooklyn Bridge?"

"Wherever you want, lady."

Everything was crystal clear in her mind. The only doubt at all was whether Jake would still be there. Her anxiety grew as the cab inched closer to the city, and she cursed her indecision that had kept her from calling him last night.

Rebecca's heart beat like the percussion section of the orchestra as she raced onto the Brooklyn Bridge. She felt his presence before she saw him. Her pace increased. He didn't see her. Jake had stopped to take pictures for a group of Japanese tourists. When they were all in position he snapped shots of them against the Manhattan skyline. He was right, the best view of city was through the spidery cables of the bridge. She was amazed that she had never noticed it before. The group handed Jake two more cameras, before shaking his hand and thanking him.

Finally the group dispersed. Jake watched them move off, to take pictures on their own. Rebecca found herself standing directly in front of Jake.

"Short trip," he said.

"Very short." She stopped to catch her breath. "I gave the tickets to another ballerina."

"How'd you know where to find me?"

"I know you better than you think, Jake Fleichman."

"And you still decided to come back."

"I didn't want to miss the view."

"What do you think of it?"

Rebecca wasn't looking at the scenery. The tenderness in his expression amazed her. "I love what I see."

"So do I." He laughed and hugged her tight.

The Japanese tourists had stopped taking pictures. They watched and waited for Jake's next move. "Just like a movie." One of the woman dabbed at her eyes.

"Why do I always feel like I'm on stage when I'm with you." Jake looked mysteriously over his shoulder. "Might as well give them the whole show."

Rebecca had no idea what he was talking about. He pulled an envelope out of his back pocket and handed it to her.

"What's this?" she asked.

"Tickets to London."

"London?" She regarded him quizzically. "You're not funny."

"I'm very serious." He placed his hand on her waist. "I had no right to expect you to turn down a chance to dance for royalty."

"No big deal." Rebecca shrugged. His touch was reassuring. She knew she had made the right decision. "I've danced for the Queen before."

"What I'm trying to say is maybe we could use these tickets." His expression stilled and grew serious. "Just the two of us. On our honeymoon."

Rebecca wasn't sure she had heard him correctly. "If you're asking me to marry you, I accept."

"You do?" Jake released a sigh of relief.

"Of course I do."

Then, to the delight of their audience, he placed his arms around her waist and pulled her close. She reached up and hugged her arms around his neck. They swayed to the sounds of the city and the beat of their hearts. With every step they took, Rebecca knew she had made the right choice. For a grand finale, Jake twirled her around the walkway. The group applauded.

Between little kisses and sobs of laughter, Rebecca managed to speak. "If I had known you were such a wonderful dancer, I might have fallen in love with you sooner."

"I loved you before I met you. Why did you take so long to show up?" He looked at her for a long moment. "Will you promise me one thing?"

"Anything," she whispered.

"Will you always save the last dance for me?"

"I wouldn't have it any other way," Rebecca said.